It's Gonna Be Alright

BY

MICHAEL JACKSON

RoseDog 🐾 Books

PITTSBURGH, PENNSYLVANIA 15222

ISBN # 0-8059-9037-2

ISBN-13 #978-0-8059-9037-9

Library of Congress Control Number: 2005930432

Printed in the United States of America
First Printing
For information or to order additional books, please write:
RoseDog Books
701 Smithfield Street, Third Floor
Pittsburgh, Pennsylvania 15222
U.S.A.
1-800-788-7654
Or visit our website and online catalogue at *www.rosedogbookstore.com*

Acknowledgements

First of all, I would like to give all of my thanks to God and to all of those people who truly care and deserve all my love. My precious, lovely, young princess, my daughter, Teaira Jackson. It's because of you, sweetheart, that I can smile today and look so forward to tomorrow...

Also, I could never forget my sister, Roberta Johnson, who stood by my side, believing me and never doubting my dreams. To Joyce Patton, you will always be my life long "sweetheart." To Donna Banks, thanks for all of your support and love.

Special thanks to two men who helped me achieve this wonderful dream of becoming an author. Mr. Charles Threat, author of *Pinstripes and Panties*. Thank you so much for all of your help. And also to my good, young friend, Jimmy DaSaint, author of *Money, Desires and Regrets*, as well as *On Everything I Love*. Thanks, Jimmy, for being the person who encouraged me to start writing my book.

To my good friend, Leo Vasquez. We both came a long way, baby, and it's gonna be alright.

Prologue

It was a hot summer morning in 1967. I was staying at the Argon Hotel on 13th Street right off Adams Street. I had four hotel rooms, three for my ho's and one for myself.

I was six deep. I'd been in the pimp game for about a year now. I was eighteen years old and feeling good about myself. I'd just gotten dressed. It was 10:30 in the morning. My ho's had been out working for a couple of hours already. It was time for me to go out on the stroll to check things out. I am always looking for that next ho to knock off.

I was standing in front of the mirror admiring myself, wearing a navy blue silk and mohair suit, navy blue gators, powder blue Italian knit sweater with the silk front. I stepped back to get a better look at myself, popped the collar of the sweater up and folded it down on top of my suit collar. I poured a little Jade East cologne into my hands, rubbed my hands together and applied it to my face and neck. Now I'm looking good and smelling just as good. My young chocolate complexion glowed under the light. My skin was as smooth as a baby's ass. I smiled, thinking to myself, I understand now why ho's are so drawn to me. Here I am, young, handsome and true to the game. I am a pimp, and a good one. I will one day be international.

I was about to leave. I picked up my two diamond rings and applied one to each pinky finger. One was a carat and the other was a five-carat cluster. I then put on my watch, which was a Lucius Pickard. It had thirty diamonds around the bezel. Now I was ready to tackle the world.

I left the hotel, walked down the street to where my canary yellow 1967 convertible Caddy was parked. I got in, turned the ignition on and dropped the top. I decided that before I went on the stroll I would go on the north side of town. I stopped at Levee's Bar on Bancroft and Franklin streets.

I went inside. There weren't that many people inside. It was still early. I was hoping that I could meet some young lady that I could add to my stable. Many young ladies are fascinated with pimps. They would never admit it to their man, but in their mind, they were curious as hell. What is it that makes a pimp any different than any other man? What is it about them that makes a woman want to sell her body, to pay them just to be with them? And how does a pimp control his dick better than any other man? Most men would have sex whenever it is offered to them. But a pimp will turn it down unless there is money in it. I would not let a bitch suck my dick if the money wasn't right, let alone fuck her. It takes a certain kind of man to pimp. It's not in everyone. You have to be able to control your sex drive like the Pied Piper played his flute and led the mice of Hamlin into the sea. A pimp plays his ho's and leads them into the sea of men to fill his pockets. No demand is outrageous. And every demand is to be met! No questions asked! A ho does as her pimp says, and that's the bottom line.

I looked over and saw my man, Juice, standing by the pool table. He called me over and asked if I wanted to shoot a few games of pool. I agreed, figuring that I'll shoot a couple of games and move on.

Juice was a good friend. He was a lot older than me. He stood about 5'10", light skinned, about twenty-seven years old and he had half of the tops of two fingers missing. They were cut off in an accident at his job. It was amazing to watch how well he shot pool, in spite of the missing fingers.

He would occasionally come by my hotel room after coming from Detroit from copping his supply of heroin. He would ask me if he could cut and bag up his dope. I would let him, because we were cool. I would always ask questions about it. Out of curiosity, I wanted to know why people liked it so much? Whenever he would leave, he would offer me a pile of dope. I would say, "No, I don't fuck with anything like that. All I do is pimp ho's and slam Cadillac doors and count money and read the funnies." He would smile and say, "Get paid, young man."

Little did I know that years down the road, I would try it for the first time and wouldn't like it. And after trying it a few more times, I would start to enjoy it. That would be the beginning of my downfall. It would take a couple of years of hell before I would start to rise again.

After shooting a few games with my friend, I decided that it was time to head for the stroll. We said our goodbyes. I left out of the bar and jumped into my Caddy and headed for Jefferson Street. It was around one o'clock.

As I cruised down Jefferson Street, ho's were coming in and out of bars on both sides of the street. As I was pulling my car inside of the parking lot next door to the Starlight Lounge, I saw Rini getting into a trick's car. She was my bottom ho. A couple other pimps were pulling up as I was exiting my car. I walked into the Starlight Lounge and saw Jackie sitting at the bar with a trick. I scanned the lounge to see if any of my other girls were there. I didn't see any of them. I decided to go down the street to the Crystal Lounge, which is located in the Milner Hotel. As I was walking into the Crystal Lounge, LaShawn was coming through the doorway with two white tricks following close behind her. She looked at me and winked. The look of lust was plastered on both men's faces. Their eyes were glued to LaShawn's sweet round ass. Both men nudged each other like it was their first piece of black ass. It may have been.

I looked around to see if I saw any of my other girls. There were none there. Maybe they were all out on dates. I was getting pretty hungry now. I decided to go down to the Lincoln Restaurant to get me something to eat. It was owned and run by this Greek man named George. Their food was decent. I ordered some veal, rice, gravy, corn and a coke to drink with my meal.

Two years later—1969...

All of the pimps and hustlers were hanging out on Jefferson Street. The traffic was thick. I had just pulled up in front of the Tenodos Lounge. It was the fall of 1969. Money was everywhere. A year earlier, Martin Luther King was assassinated. Jefferson Street was shut down. They rioted in most of the cities in the United States.

As I stepped from my car, I heard someone call me. "Mark, baby!"

I turned to see who it was. It was Memphis Slim. He was a young pimp that just got in town a year ago. "What's up, baby?" How's pimpin'?" I asked.

"Good, Mark, it couldn't be better. Ho's are humping their asses off. Getting my paper right. I just knocked off two new ho's since I last saw you, Mark."

"That's good, baby. Come on in, Slim, let me buy you a drink."

Slim was a smooth, young pimp. He had a lot of class about himself. He stood 6'4" and was very dark.

As we headed toward the bar, a car horn blew. It was three of my girls. They pulled over to the curb. I turned to Slim and told him that I would be there in a minute.

I walked over to the car. Jackie said, "Daddy, your girls have been working hard all day."

Jackie was my bottom ho. She was the foundation that held my stable together when I'm not around. Each one of my girls pulled out their individual rolls of money and handed them to me through the open window.

"Penny, did you get the six suits that I wanted?" Penny was my booster girl. She also worked the stroll.

"Yes, Daddy, they are at home. The ones that you wanted and a few extra ones as well."

"Good, baby. You all can go back to work. I'll see you girls later."

After the girls drove off, I went inside the bar. I ordered a cherry coke and Slim a double Hennessey with Coke on the side. We shot a couple games of pool. We then sat at the bar and I bought us another round of drinks.

We kicked the game around a while. After finishing our drinks, we shook hands and went our separate ways. I then decided to go across the street to the Greyhound bus station. As I was walking through, I noticed this beautiful, high yellow complexioned woman with a sandy colored Afro, with big brown eyes. She was absolutely gorgeous. She stood about 5'4".

I quickly introduced myself. "Hello, beautiful. My name is Mark. What is yours?"

She gave me a stare.

I said, "I'm sorry. I know it's not proper to approach a stranger like this, but believe me, sweetheart, I am harmless. I just want to get to know you."

"Joyce is my name," she smiled.

"Pleased to meet you, Joyce. I see that you have your suitcase. Are you coming or going?"

"I'm not from around here. My bus is laid over and I was trying to make a phone call for someone to come and pick me up."

"I see. I wish that you could stay in our city overnight. That way I could get to know you better. There are a few nice hotels down the street from here, and if you don't have the extra money, I will gladly pay for it for you."

"That is so sweet of you, Mark, but I need to get home. Do you have change for a dollar? I need to make a call."

I reached in my pocket and gave her the change that she needed to make the call and told her to keep her dollar. I then said that I hope that no one is at home in a jokingly manner and smiled. She smiled back. She put the change in the phone and dialed the number. After a few unsuccessful attempts to reach someone, she finally gave up.

"Your hopes came true," she said.

"Then let me take you and show you around the city. I'll put your suitcase in a locker until we come back. Have you eaten anything yet? If not, then we can stop and get something."

She was hesitant at first. She looked deep into my eyes. I can't tell you to this day what she saw, but she decided to come with me.

I needed to take her as far from the bus station as possible. I needed time to capture this beautiful woman's confidence and trust in me as well as her heart. I took her to meet my older sister, Marie, with whom I am very close. To my amazement, the two of them hit if off instantly! And it all played out perfectly.

That day was the beginning of many wonderful dreams to follow. I was on top of my game. I didn't get high off of anything but money.

To realize a dream is to lose it. But to lose a dream and to recover it is amazing! But in my heart, I knew "It's gonna be alright!"

Chapter One

Two years later, the winter of 1971...

Joyce and I had gotten out early. My Jones was kicking my ass. I needed to make some money. I decided to take Joyce to a few stores in hopes of coming up with some decent pieces and get this monkey off my back and build my bankroll up at the same time.

It was a bitter cold morning. The snow was coming down thick, covering my windshield. I switched on my wipers. My mind drifted back to a few years ago on how well I was doing. Since then, I had gone through several stables of ho's. Now I was down to just Joyce.

She'd been with me ever since 1969 when I met her in the bus station. I was jerked out of my thoughts when Joyce spoke out. "Baby, are you alright?"

"Yes, sweetheart. Why'd you ask?

"Because it seems as if you were in another world, and I didn't want you to get into no accident. It's pretty bad out here."

"I was just thinking about where we could go next. We had been to a couple of malls already and hadn't broke luck yet. And I don't know how much longer I can take this here. I am aching all over. I need some blow!"

"Mark, what about Westgate Shopping Center? We haven't gone there yet."

"Okay, we're not that far from there. Let's go and see what happens."

As I headed for Westgate Shopping Center, I was thinking to myself, what a hell of a woman I have. She don't fuck with none of this shit.

As I was pulling my 1970 Cadillac into the shopping center, I decided to cruise past all of the stores first. As I was passing Diamonds Men's Store, Joyce said, "Baby, park here and let me try Diamonds."

I pulled deep enough into the parking lot to camouflage my car from the store. I parked. Joyce reached over the back seat and grabbed the shop box. She looked at me and said, "Okay, baby, let's see what happens." She opened the door and exited the car.

I was sitting there with my nose running and my joints aching, hoping that she would come up this time. So far, we had nothing but buzzard luck.

Fifteen minutes later, she returned. Joyce opened the car door and lay the shop box on the front seat. I pulled the box over closer to me as she was getting in. It was still snowing and large snowflakes accompanied her into the car as she tucked her long brown leather maxi coat underneath her.

"Was you able to come up, baby?" I asked her.

"Yes, Daddy. I managed to get five men's leather coats."

"Beautiful, sweetheart. Now where do you plan on going?"

"Well, baby, on my way to Diamonds I was walking past Toledo Furs and it really looked cool inside. I think that I'll go and check it out and see if I can get some of those beautiful furs."

"If you can come up with two or three of those, I think that we can call it a day. Baby, hurry up, my bowels are about to break."

"I'll try to make it fast, Daddy." She then opened the door to get out.

"Baby, I'm getting weak and I'm really sick."

"I know, sweetheart. I'll be right back."

I reached under the seat and grabbed a large black garbage bag and put the leather coats in it. Joyce got back out with the shop box.

We always use a shop box around Christmas time. We can get more pieces at one time that way. It was a big box, gift wrapped like a present with a big bow on top. And a drop bottom that you can drop clothes in.

Twenty minutes had passed since Joyce left. I sat squirming in my seat, sick and very uncomfortable, as I kept an eye on the front door of Toledo Furs waiting for Joyce.

I hit the dashboard of the car. "Damn it! Where is she?" My nose was running and my joints were still aching. I was in serious pain. I reached into my pocket and pulled out my soiled handkerchief and blew my nose. My stomach was bubbling even more so. I needed to find a bathroom. Fast! At that moment, I saw Joyce walking toward the car. She was moving swiftly. She got in the car and said, "Baby, drive! Hurry!"

"Baby, is everything alright?" I asked her.

"I'm not sure if this little old lady saw me or not."

As I was pulling out of the shopping center, I asked, "What did you get?"

"I got two full length mink coats and a chinchilla cape."

"Check the price tags on the minks."

"They are both four thousand, six hundred dollars apiece."

"What about the cape?"

"It's twelve hundred, Daddy."

I managed to smile through the pain and leaned over and kissed Joyce. "You did good, baby. You did real good."

At that moment, Joyce screamed out, "Baby, look out!"

I jerked the steering wheel hard to the right. I stomped on the brakes. The big Caddy slipped up onto the curb and into a telephone post. I went to get out of the car. The door was hitting against the fender. I pushed hard and the door opened. I looked over at Joyce. "Are you alright, baby.

She looked back at me. "I'm fine, sweetheart."

Then I stepped from the car. The right fender was crushed. It dug into the tire. The car wasn't going anywhere.

"Damn it!" I kicked the tire. I looked up the street. The car that caused me this misery was long gone. I took the bags with the furs and leather coats and put them in the trunk.

We walked to the nearest phone booth and called a tow truck and went back to the car. Thirty minutes later, the tow truck arrived. We rode with the tow truck driver back to the dealer's and picked up a rental. We'd have to have a car to make money. We were given a little red Corvair as a rental. We put our bags in the trunk. The Caddy wouldn't be ready for at least two weeks or more, they said.

I continued to complain as I drove to Mitch's house. Mitch pays the best for furs. Most fences gave a third, but Mitch gave us $4,000 for $10,400 worth of furs. A fence was someone who bought "hot items" and always paid cash. Now, I can finally get my much needed blow.

Later that night, as we lay in bed, Joyce and I were talking after a long bout of lovemaking.

"You know, sweetheart, maybe we need to go to a new city? Hustling is getting a little difficult here. And this Jones is kicking my ass. I hate the day that I started fucking with this shit! Waking up sick every morning. I remember the time when I didn't have no habit and was all about money! Everything seems to be going wrong now. It's just one thing after another. I think it's time for a change, baby. Maybe a new city or something. I wish that I'd never started fucking with this heroin. I didn't understand what I was getting myself into. This shit has brought me down. And I hate having to depend on dope just to get moving everyday."

Joyce snuggled up close to me. "Baby, let me give my sister, Donna, a call tomorrow, in Lansing, Michigan and ask if we could come and stay with her for a while until we could get ourselves together."

"That sounds good, baby. Anywhere but this town. Maybe my luck would change. And maybe I could gradually wean myself off of this shit."

I then kissed my beautiful woman. She was always there and always down with me. No matter what! And I loved her for that! A man needs a good woman that's going to be there for him through the good and the bad. I pulled Joyce even closer to me and gave her another kiss and said goodnight. Then we both drifted off to sleep.

The next morning, Joyce called her sister and she agreed to let us come and stay with her until we got ourselves together. A week later, we turned in the rental car and packed up a U-Haul and headed to Lansing. Once we arrived, we set up our furniture in Donna's huge basement where we would be living.

Our money was tight. After two weeks of spending, I didn't have much money left from the furs. I counted my roll. I had eight hundred dollars. Just enough to get my car out of the shop, once it was fixed.

I suggested to Joyce that she see if she could get her sister's car so that we could go out shortchanging. I could use the extra money because the "monkey" was still on my back. Actually, it was kicking my ass!

Joyce asked her sister if it would be alright if we borrowed her car for awhile because I wanted to get acquainted with Lansing. But the real reason was that my sickness was coming down on me.

Donna suggested that we go down on Butler Street. There was a community center, a bar-b-que joint and a poolroom where a lot of young adults like ourselves hung out. We said that we would check it out, then we left.

We rode around, stopping at several restaurants and gas stations across the city. Shortchanging.

After making three hundred extra dollars, I decided to go down on Butler Street to see if I could find me a connection for some dope.

The first place that we stopped was the community center. Donna was right. There were quite a few young adults hanging out in there.

As we were walking through the place, many eyes were focused on us. We were both extremely sharp. Joyce had on a long forest green maxi suede coat with a two-piece suede outfit on underneath. I was wearing a brown leather maxi with a two-piece leather and knit outfit underneath.

We were new to the set, and the look of wondering who we were was on many faces. After standing around for ten minutes or so, a tall, jet-black man came into the center. Everybody in the place greeted this sharply dressed man with great respect. It kinda reminded me of when I was on top of my game.

Everybody in the place seemed to like him. He had this certain charisma about him. I wondered who the man was that everyone seemed to like.

I walked over to the man with the celebrity status. "Excuse me, my friend, my name is Mark." I extended my hand and said, "I'm not from around here."

He accepted my handshake and said, "My name is Tony. Where are you from, Mark?"

"I'm from Ohio. This is my woman, Joyce."

"Pleased to meet you, Joyce."

"Pleased to meet you too, Tony."

"Are you here visiting?" Tony asked.

"No, we just moved here. We are staying with my woman's sister until we can find our own place."

As we were talking, I kept sniffling and my eyes were watering. "Mark, are you Jonesing?" Tony asked.

I answered in a low tone, "Yes. I'm pretty sick. I was hoping to find something. But by me not knowing anybody, I didn't know where to start."

"What do you need, Mark?"

"Whatever a hundred dollars can get me."

"Come on. I'll take you to where you can get straightened out."

We left the center. We trudged through the snow to our car. We all got in. Tony directed me where to go. Five minutes into the ride, we pulled in front of a big white house with a wire fence going around it. I reached into my pocket and pulled out my roll and peeled off a hundred dollars and handed it to Tony.

He then opened the door and exited the car. He walked to the fence, opened the gate and walked through it. Then he went around to the back of the house.

After sitting nervously waiting for Tony, he appeared from the back out of the darkness and walked back to the car. He got in and handed me the package. I asked him if it was alright for me to hit it before we pulled off.

"Go ahead, Mark."

I opened the package and was amazed at how big the package was. I instantly thought that it was garbage. I immediately inserted two large scoops up my nose and folded the package back up.

I started the engine and asked Tony if he wanted me to drop him back off at the center.

"No, you can drop me off at home." He directed me to his house. As I was driving, I was thinking to myself, "He done gave me some garbage!"

All of a sudden, out of nowhere, the dope hit me. The shit was good! It was damn good!

I pulled in front of Tony's house. We sat in the car talking for about twenty minutes, getting better acquainted. I really liked this guy. I told him that I would stop by the next day. I thanked him and asked what I owed him?

"You don't owe me anything, Mark. I was glad I could help."

"I wasn't always like this, Tony. I'm getting ready to quit. We moved here for a new start."

"If there is anything that I can do to help, let me know, Mark."

After Tony exited the car, Joyce and I went on back to the house.

"He seems cool, baby," Joyce said.

"Yeah, I like him. I really like the guy."

Later that night...

Joyce and I lay in bed. My mood was the best that Joyce had seen in months. The new environment and the heroin that I had in my system had a lot to do with it. We talked for quite a while about the past and about our future. I told her that I needed to get off of this shit. She boosted my ego by saying that anything that I set my mind to do, I can do. She said that she had seen me do it too many times in the past.

"Baby, I'm tired of going out the world backwards. Here we are, baby, steadily making good money. And I'm fucking it up just as fast as we make it. I don't want to go to a hospital. So when I see Tony tomorrow, I'll ask him if he knows anybody selling Methadone. Baby, I need to clean up in order to come up."

"Don't you worry, honey, it's gonna be alright, and no matter what, I'll be here by your side," Joyce said, snuggling up under my arms. "You always got me, Mark. Always!"

The next morning...

I went by Tony's house, parked in the driveway and walked up onto the porch. I rang the doorbell. I heard the latch click and the door swung open. On the other side of the door stood Tony with a big smile on his face.

"Come on in, Mark," he said as if we'd been friends for many years.

I stepped through the door. We walked into the living room and both sat down.

"How are you doing, Mark?"

"I feel better now that I got some shit in me. But the thing is, Tony, this is not me. What I'm saying is that there was a time that all I did was make money and live the good life. I got introduced to this stuff a couple of years ago. I had no idea the effect that it would have on me down the line. This thing has destroyed my life and I need to get it back. What I'm saying is that I want to get off of this shit. Do you know anyone that sells Methadone?"

"Not right off hand. What about going into a hospital, Mark?"

"No! I don't like hospitals. I never did. I may have to do this by myself. There is nothing harder than to kick a heroin habit. I have a good woman in my corner. She has always been there for me. This is not the life I wanted for her, or for myself. I know I will be in much pain, vomiting and sweating profusely. My bones will ache like hell and I will wish I was dead, but I'm willing to go through all of this just to get this poison out of my system."

Tony paused and looked me straight in my eyes then said, "Mark, I feel you and if there is anything I can do, I'm here for you."

"Thanks, Tony, thanks," I said shaking his hand.

That day was the beginning of Tony and my friendship. I went back home and called my sister Marie. She asked how I was doing. "I'm alright. I just need to get this monkey off my back and get back to 100 percent. I'm going to come up one day, Sis, and I will take good care of you. You won't want for anything."

"Mark, all I want is for you to get yourself back to the way that you were, clean and free from that junk," Marie said.

"I will, Sis. I love you. Bye."

"Bye, Mark, take care of yourself."

I then hung up.

It would take another two weeks living in my nightmare of hell before I decide to kick this monkey that's been riding my back for the last couple of years. No! I have it wrong. It had become a gorilla!

I would no longer allow myself to be the victim of the brown powder that has claimed so many!

Chapter Two

Two weeks later...

I was just waking up. I looked as bad as I felt. It had been a long hard fight, but I'd won. No more sickness. No shakes, no sweating. Nothing. Joyce had nursed me through it all. She'd cleaned up my mess, applied cold towels to my head, she'd done it all.

She was now in the kitchen cooking breakfast for me. I'd gotten my appetite back and was feeling a lot better. The smell of the bacon frying in the skillet helped push me along.

By the time I'd showered and gotten dressed, my plate was on the table in front of me. I devoured all of my food. I washed up and put on a tan colored jumpsuit. Joyce picked out my Afro for me. As she stood there admiring her handsome man, she said, "Now that's the Mark that I know and love." She put her arms around my neck and kissed me gently.

I checked my bankroll. I counted up the little bit of money that I had. "Damn baby, we need to go make some money." I only had two hundred and twenty dollars.

Joyce got dressed and again asked Donna if we could use her car. Donna never said no. She was glad that I was up and feeling better.

Joyce sat in the car as I went into the store. I walked around as the clerk finished up with a customer. The clerk looked up at me.

"Hello, sir." I was always courteous.

"Hello," the clerk said. "How can I help you?"

"Sir, would you do me a favor? I've got all of these small bills and I was wondering if you could give me a twenty dollar bill for 3 fives and 5 ones."

The clerk opened the cash register and checked his large bills. "Yes, sir, I can do that for you."

I counted out 3 five dollar bills and then the one dollar bills. The clerk handed me the twenty and started counting out the money as he placed it in the drawer. I turned and slowly started walking toward the door.

"Excuse me, sir," the clerk called out. "Excuse me, but you are short."

I turned and walked back to the counter. I counted out the money. It totaled nineteen dollars. "I'm sorry, you are right, sir." I reached into my front pocket and pulled out my roll of money. I peeled off a dollar bill and added it to the money that the clerk had laid on the counter.

I counted it out slowly. "Five, ten, fifteen, sixteen, seventeen, eighteen, nineteen, and twenty." I then added the twenty dollar bill to the pile of bills and pushed it all toward the clerk.

"Just give me 4 tens instead."

The clerk picked up the pile of money and counted out loud. "Twenty, twenty-five, thirty, thirty-five and 5 ones is forty." The clerk then gave me 4 ten dollar bills. I thanked him and calmly walked out of the store.

Once I was inside the car, Joyce asked, "How'd it go, baby?"

"Fine, it went fine, baby. That clerk is still proud of the fact that he didn't allow me to beat him out of a dollar."

We both laughed aloud. We drove around pulling the con on several more stores. I then decided that we had enough money. We pulled over to a phone booth and I called Tony. Joyce had suggested that we all hang out tonight. We agreed to meet at Tony's house at 7 o'clock.

At 7 o'clock we pulled up in front of Tony's house. The yard was full of snow. The walk was freshly shoveled. We walked up to the door. I stood back and admired the house. "One day we are gonna have a house like this."

Joyce gave my hand a squeeze. I rang the doorbell. A cute young lady of about eighteen years old opened the door. "Can I help you?" she politely asked.

"Yes, is Tony home? He was expecting us. Tell him Mark is here."

The young girl let us in, closed the door and ran after Tony. I gazed around the living room. Nice. Real nice.

Tony came into the living room. He stopped and took a real long look at me. That big, bright smile flashed across his face. He shook his head. "My man. My man, you sure look good, man. Real good." Tony walked up and embraced me. He held me for a while.

"Who are these nice looking people?"

Tony released me. He stepped back. "Oh, hi, Mom. Mom, this is my friend, Mark, and his girlfriend, Joyce."

I walked up and kissed Tony's mother on the cheek. Joyce did too. "I'm glad to meet you, Mrs. Moore," I said.

A short extremely pretty light-skinned lady came into the room. She walked over and put her arm around Tony. Tony eased her around so that everybody could see her. "Hi, everybody," she said.

He smiled and said, "This is my beautiful woman, Brenda." Tony and Brenda got their coats. We said our goodbyes to Mrs. Moore and we all left.

"I hope that you know a good restaurant to go to. I am starving."

"Is there anything special that you'd like to eat, Mark?"

"I'd like to have a nice big steak myself. Joyce, what about you, baby? Is there anything special that you want?"

"Baby, a steak is good with me."

"Is that alright with you all?"

"Sure, it's cool with us. Then we will go to the steakhouse down on Columbus Street. You are gonna really love the Texas Toast that they have there, Mark."

"Hungry as I am, I'm going to enjoy a good meal right now. I've been having a hell of an appetite lately."

"I'll bet you have," said Tony. Tony and Joyce both started laughing.

Brenda was sitting there with a puzzled look on her face. "Let me in on the joke," she said.

"I guess they are going to keep it to themselves, Brenda."

Then I looked in the rear view mirror at Tony. "How do I get to the steakhouse, Tony?"

He gave me directions. I started the car and off we went. We all were having a good time, talking and listening to the radio. I pulled in front of the steakhouse. Then we all got out and went inside.

It seems that everybody in the place knew Tony. He would introduce me to everyone as his cousin from out of town. It must have taken us ten minutes to be seated after talking to so many people in the restaurant.

After going through the menu, I decided that not only would I order a steak, but I ordered a lobster tail as well. I wanted to try out the Texas Toast, so I ordered two of them.

Joyce ordered the same as I did and Brenda and Tony did too, except for the lobster tail.

The girls excused themselves to go to the restroom. As soon as they left, Tony leaned over to me and said, "Now that you are clean, what is your plan?"

I painted Tony a brief picture of my life before I got hooked on these drugs. I told him that I had started pimping at the age of eighteen. I had a stable of six ho's. Through the years I had copped and blown many ho's.

"I had never worked before in my life. All I know is to pimp. So I guess that I'll try and build me a stable now that I'm clean.

He asked if Joyce was one of my working girls. I told him yes. I had knocked Joyce off in 1969. I was seven deep then. Joyce was a square and I turned her out.

"She had been down with me through many cops and blows. As you can see, Joyce is the only one that I have left. I lost all of them once I got strung out on the shit."

"But you are crazy about Joyce, aren't you?"

"Tony, you know that a pimp is not supposed to fall in love with his ho's. But I have to tell you that I love Joyce."

"Mark, I really dig you. I've got a lot of friends, but there is something about you that is so different. I want to pull your coat to something. And if you like what I say, you don't have to pimp no more. You can become a millionaire."

"Tony, you have my undivided attention. I'm listening." That's when he ran it down.

He said, "I'm getting ready to come into a large shipment of heroin. I know this guy. We are real cool and he's waiting on a shipment from Mexico. It should be here any time now. And he's going to let me have as much as I want on consignment for as long as I want it. I dig you, Mark, and I know that you are a solid brother. I want you to be my partner. I want you to be with me all the way."

"Are you serious, Tony?"

"I'm as serious as a heart attack, and that's pretty damned serious. Are you with me?"

I looked him straight in the eyes. "Tony, I'm your man. I'm with you. Just let me know when you're ready."

"Cool, baby," Tony said.

"Cool."

The waitress came with our food. The girls came back right after the waitress had left. The food was great and so was the conversation. The four of us got along great. Brenda mentioned that the club down the street featured live entertainers.

We rode down the street and got front row seats. Joyce and Brenda both got a little tipsy. The group that performed was a local group. They sang all of the Temptations greatest hits. We all had a wonderful time.

When the club closed, we dropped Tony and Brenda off at Tony's house. Joyce slid up under my arms as I drove home.

This is how it was supposed to be, my woman and me enjoying life. This was beautiful. Joyce was feeling pretty good. All I had to drink was cherry coke. I always had extra cherries put into my glass. But I was feeling high on life. My mind was clear now and I was focusing on how I could get more money.

As I undressed for bed, I was watching Joyce undress. Her beautiful smooth, red bone complexion, her firm round behind, her thick thighs. I watched her completely undress and lay on the bed.

I finished undressing and lay on the bed next to her. We started kissing. My hands went to those firm round ass cheeks. I kissed her breasts slowly, rolling my tongue across her nipples. I kissed my way down her flat stomach. I kissed each thigh. Then I lightly lifted her behind and placed a pillow under her. I licked the softness in the middle bush. She opened herself wide for me. I licked like a hungry puppy would lap a bowl of milk.

She moaned aloud and thrashed her head from side to side. Her entire body quivered when she came. She pushed me back onto the bed and gently began to suck my rock hard dick. I lifted her up and we got into a 69 position.

Joyce was really getting loud, even with my dick in her mouth. Finally I put the pillow under her ass again, only this time, I placed the head of my dick into her tight wet pussy. We fucked like that for quite a while. Joyce got louder and louder. Her moans and sounds were really turning me on even more.

When I came, she came again. She squealed.

Donna was knocking on her floor. Joyce and I started laughing. We slept like that, holding each other tight.

The next day we went by Tony's house. His cute little sister answered the door. She yawned as if she'd been up all night. "Tony's not here," she said. "He's in the hospital. Mama had to rush him there last night."

"The hospital!" I was shocked. We were just laughing and having a good time last night."

His sister yawned again. "They said he has walking pneumonia. He could hardly breath last night."

"What hospital is he in?" I asked.

"Lansing General Hospital."

"Thanks, sweetheart." We turned and walked away.

I drove to the hospital as fast as I could without getting a ticket. When we walked into the hospital room, Tony seemed so small. He had tubes in his nose. He wheezed really bad when he spoke.

I was really worried. We'd become good friends. I was at the hospital every day until he came home. Anything that he wanted, I got for him. Dozens of people came to see Tony. He was a very popular guy. But nobody stayed as long as I did. And none of the things that they did for him meant as much as the things that I did for him. He was my main man. It was six long days before Tony came home, but we were all glad when he did.

Chapter Three

Two months later...spring time 1971

Joyce, Tony, Brenda and I had been going out quite a lot over the last two months.

The phone rang. I answered it. "Hello."

"Hey, baby, this is Tony. What you got up for tonight?"

"Nothing, what's up with you?"

"Brenda was wondering what you and Joyce were doing for the night? Did y'all want to hang out or something?"

"That sounds cool, but I hate having to keep asking Donna for her car. Damn, I wish that I had my Caddy."

There was a pause for a minute then Tony said, "I didn't know that you had a Cadillac."

"Yeah, man, I had a 1970 Cadillac, but I wrecked it right before we moved up here."

"How much does it cost to get it out of the shop?"

"Man, it will cost too much. I owe for the damages and I'm four months behind on the note."

Again, it got quiet on Tony's end of the phone.

"Mark, be patient. Remember what we talked about a little while back. Be patient, baby. So what about tonight?"

I took a deep breath. "Yeah, baby, what time?

"Make it about 6 o'clock. Let's get an early start."

"Cool, Tony, I'll see you then," and I hung up.

I went back to where Joyce was sitting on the edge of the bed. "Get dressed really pretty for me, baby. I want to go out and have a real good time tonight.

We got Donna's car and picked up Tony and Brenda. Tony was as clean as the board of health. He had on a white suit that fit like it was tailor made. His real dark complexion seemed to glow against the suit.

Brenda wore a white miniskirt with a white ruffled blouse. They made a very good looking couple.

I wore a powder blue two-piece outfit, bell bottoms and a waistcoat. On my feet I wore a pair of blue turtles. Joyce wore a powder blue mini that complimented my outfit.

We drove down to the Capitol Park Hotel. They had a real nice club inside. We went inside and had a couple of drinks. I drank my regular cherry coke with extra cherries. The place was jumping. It was full of young people like ourselves.

After a couple of hours, we decided to go back over to the club that had the local entertainment. Club Cocoa. We were lucky. We got the same seats that we'd had before. There were a couple of groups here this time. A group that sounded like the O'Jays and a female group that imitated the Supremes.

Joyce really liked the club. She liked it a lot. I looked around. The stage was nice. Not new, but nice. The carpeting was a little worn. The tables and the chairs seemed solid. I had to agree with her. This was a nice club.

The female group came onto the stage. They wore long sequined dresses and had tall wigs on their heads. The music started. They raised their hands. "Stop! in the name of love, before you break my heart."

I looked over and Brenda and Joyce were swaying to the music while singing the classic song. I almost hated when the club finally closed. We were having such a great time. We went to breakfast at the International House of Pancakes on Logan Street.

At 4:30, the night was finally over and I drove Tony and Brenda home, then we proceeded home.

One week later...

I was just finishing supper when the phone rang. Joyce answered it. "Hello. Just a moment. Baby, telephone."

"Hello," I said, taking the phone.

"What's happening, my man?"

"Hey, Tony, what's up, baby?"

"Mark, do you remember what we talked about?"

"What we talked about?" I thought for a moment. "Yeah, yeah, I remember," I said.

"Then come on over here. I'm waiting for you."

"I'm on my way, baby." I hung up the phone, turned and hugged Joyce. "Go get the car keys, baby. That package that Tony been waiting on has come in."

Joyce hugged me again. I smiled and looked down at her. "It's gonna be alright now, baby. It's gonna be alright."

Joyce went and got the keys. I kissed her goodbye. I cruised on over to Tony's. I knocked on the door and waited. Tony opened the door and stood back with a big grin on his face. "Come on in, baby."

I smiled back as I followed him inside.

"Come on, we are going to go down into the basement. We can take care of our business down there." The basement was Tony's sanctuary.

I followed him down the stairs and over to a coffee table that was sitting in front of a large couch. On the coffee table sat a pound of heroin.

I sat down on the couch. "Damn, baby! We're getting ready to make some serious money. How much more of this can you get?"

"As much as we need, Mark, there's no limit!"

"It looks like it's some good shit and it smells strong."

"This shit is good. My connection is getting it straight out of Mexico."

"So, you still want me to be your partner one hundred percent?"

"I was serious when I asked you about it in the restaurant, Mark, and I'm still serious now. I am not one to switch up on my partner. I say what I mean and I mean what I say! You are my man. It's me and you against the world."

"I'm with that all the way, Tony."

"We're going to take over this whole city, Mark. We're going to blow up and keep on blowing up."

"What kind of cut can this take?" I was curious about what we could put on it.

Tony smiled and said, "This shit is good. It can take a fifteen. But we are only going to put a five on it."

"To do what you want to do, Tony, we are going to need a crew. And a damn good one at that."

"You're right, baby. And I've got the right men for the job. These men I can depend on. I grew up with all of them. They all have heart, and they can be ruthless. But they all are loyal to me, and they will be to you, as well. Just about everybody here in Lansing knows you as my cousin from out of town. And they know how I feel about my family. They will respect you and treat you as they treat me. With that said, we can go and pick them up now and put this thing together. But first, we're going to have to get a tester to test it with a five on it. I want this shit so damn good when it hits the street that no one else can sell their dope."

"Do you know a good tester, Tony?"

"I have this guy in mind. We call him Junky Marv."

Tony walked over to the cabinet on the other side of the room and got some aluminum foil out of it, came back over and sat next to me. He tore two good size pieces of foil off. He then took a playing card and scooped up a nice piece of heroin and placed it on the foil and asked me to fold it up. He then emptied some lactose out of a large jar and did the same. He took the bag that the pound of heroin was in and put it in a metal box and locked it. He walked over and placed it in the cabinet. "Let's go and find my men now."

I got up and we left the house. We got in the car and Tony directed me as to where to go.

We stopped up on the set. The spring weather had brought everybody out. The sidewalks were packed with people.

I pulled up to the curb. We sat in the car for a while scanning our surroundings. Tony spotted Dollar Bill standing on the porch of the bar-b-que joint. He called him over to the car.

Dollar Bill leaned into the window. "What's up, Tony? What's up, Mark? How are y'all doing?"

"We're good, Dollar Bill," Tony said. "I'm ready to start rolling. Where is everyone?"

Dollar Bill's eyes lit up with excitement. He whispered in a low voice. "It's here?"

"Yeah and I need for you to get all of the fellas together."

"Well, they are all around here somewhere. I'll go and gather them up. You want Curtis, Eugene, Tommy and Jerome, right?"

"That's right. Can we all meet at your house in about twenty minutes?"

"Sure, no problem."

At that moment, Eugene happened to walk up to the car. "Tony, what's up? Hey, Mark."

"Damn, where was you at a minute ago, Eugene?" Tony asked.

"I was across the street at the community center. On my way out, I saw you and Mark sitting here so I decided to come on over and holler at you."

"I'm glad that you came. I was just sending Dollar Bill out to look for you, Curtis, Tommy and Jerome. My shit is here and I'm ready to roll. Find the rest of the fellas and meet me at Dollar Bill's house in twenty minutes. Has anyone seen Junky Marvin? I need him to test some shit for me."

"Yeah, he was down here about a half an hour ago," Eugene said. "He's probably down at the park over on Saginow Street. He likes hanging out down there a lot."

"Alright. We are going down there to see if we can spot him. We will meet you all at the house."

Dollar Bill and Eugene stepped back from the car. I started my engine and pulled off from the curb in search of Junky Marvin.

I turned to Tony and said, "They are all fired up and ready to get down."

"They are all thoroughbreds, Mark."

We drove over on Saginow Street looking for Junky Marvin. It only took a few minutes before we found him stretched out on a park bench under a big tree. I blew my horn. He looked up. Tony waved him over to the car. He gave Marvin the run down on what we needed him to do. He immediately opened the car door and jumped into the back seat.

We headed to Dollar Bill's house. We pulled up and parked behind Dollar Bill's Buick LaSabre. Then we all exited the car and walked up to his apartment building. We climbed four flights of stairs that led to his apartment.

Marvin was complaining about all of the flights of stairs and about how sick he was. "This better be worth it," he said complaining.

Tony knocked on Dollar Bill's door. We heard footsteps coming, then the latch clicked on the door. The door swung open. Dollar Bill stepped back and said, "Come on in, fellas."

We walked in. Everybody was there just as Tony had instructed. Tony didn't waste any time. He laid the dope on the table, stepping on it five times. Junky Marvin pulled out his works and his cooker and set them on the table.

Tony dumped a small amount of dope in Marvin's cooker. We all watched as Marvin cooked up the dope and drew it up into his syringe. He then took off his belt and tied it around his arm. As his veins appeared, he inserted the needle into his arm. He pulled the blood into the syringe and shot the dope into his arm. He went into a light nod, and started scratching all over. He constantly wiped at his nose. "Damn, man! This shit is good." He fell into a deeper nod.

We kept nudging Marvin, asking him if he was alright. He would come to and say, "I'm alright. I'm just high as hell."

We all laughed. Eugene said, "If you would have given him any more, he would have killed his fool self."

We all laughed again. Tony stepped forward and told Marvin that he had to leave now. He gave him a nice pile of dope to take with him. Marvin got up and immediately left.

"Alright, it's time to get down to business. Mark is my partner and this is the way that we are going to do this. To start off, all of you will get a ten thousand dollar package. We are making Eugene our lieutenant. You will pick up and turn in to him. If there are any problems, get in touch with Eugene and he will get in touch with us. Tomorrow at noon, all of your packages will be ready. You will be able to pick them up at Eugene's house. Out of each ounce, we want a thousand dollars. And you can put a stand up two on it, and it will still be the best shit in town. My plan is to take this whole city over. Each one of you has a chance of becoming 'nigger rich.' Mark, is there anything that you want to say to the fellas?"

"No, Tony. I think that you have covered everything, and like you said, they are all thoroughbreds and I'm sure that they all know how to move this shit. I just have one suggestion. I think that once we get rolling, we need to rent a few houses to roll out of, then for the fellas to be out in the street. Each one of them then needs to get their own workers and control their own houses. And they all will be lieutenants under Eugene. Now this can only happen when we start making some serious money. I'm talking about some serious paper. With that we can get out of here, if there is nothing else, Tony."

"My cousin, Mark, has a good point. So tomorrow, after you get your package, get out there and throw down. Any questions?"

No one had any questions, so Tony said, "We're out of here."

We made a few other stops. Then I went back to Tony's house to help him bag up some packages. We worked until two in the morning and then I went home.

Joyce was asleep when I walked into the bedroom. She woke up as I got into the bed. "How did it go, baby?"

"Great, baby, everything went great. Go back to sleep." I put my arms around her and kissed her. Then I drifted off to sleep.

Chapter Four

That next morning, I woke up with Joyce lying in my arms. She looked so sweet. I kissed my beautiful woman and watched as she shifted from my arms.

As I got up to take a shower, I started thinking to myself, it's your time to shine, Mark, and now it's time to step up and make things happen. I had always been a good hustler and a leader, and now it was my time to flourish in this game.

By the time that I had gotten out of the shower, Joyce was up and cooking breakfast. She was dancing to the music that was playing on the radio.

I yelled out to her, "Good morning, sweetheart," and she answered back with a smile, and a "Good morning, handsome." I smiled back and went to the bedroom to get dressed.

After getting dressed, I came out and sat down at the kitchen table. While we were eating breakfast, Joyce asked me to tell her about last night. I told her that Tony got his shit in and we were getting ready to roll today at noon. "Everyone will pick up their packages and hit the streets."

"Baby, be careful. It's dangerous out there."

"I know, baby, but don't worry, I'll be alright."

The phone rang. Joyce walked over and picked up the phone. "Hello."

"Good morning, Joyce, this is Tony."

"Good morning to you, Tony. I'll go and get Mark for you."

"Baby, it's Tony on the phone."

"Alright, he must be ready." I walked over and took the phone. "Hey, baby, what's up, Tony? Are you ready?"

"Yeah. How long will it take you to get here?"

"About fifteen minutes. I'm leaving now."

Joyce put her hand on mine, "Baby, ask Tony if Brenda is there."

"Is Brenda there? Joyce wants to talk to her." I handed the phone to Joyce, picked up the car keys, kissed her and left out of the house.

On my way to Tony's house, I stopped at the store and ran in and picked up a Pepsi Cola. I hopped back into the car and headed for Tony's.

Ten minutes later, I pulled up in front of Tony's house and blew the horn. He came out and got into the car.

"Eugene had come by and picked up all of the packages that we had bagged up last night. Everyone will pick up their package from him around noon."

"Did you take anything by Margo's yet?"

"No, that's what this is," and he held up a bag.

"Is that the rest of the ten thousand dollar packages that we bagged up last night?"

"No, it's not Mark. This is the raw dope and some lactose. I think we need to show Margo how to cut it and bag it up. That way, she can have everything ready for Eugene when he's ready to pick up."

"Sounds good." Then I pulled off. Tony gave me directions to Margo's house. I haven't seen the little cutie pie since Tony introduced her to me a month ago. I asked Tony if she had a man? He said that she was single. I was thinking to myself maybe I would kick it with her. I'll see. It's plenty of time for that. Right now, it's all about business.

Tony interrupted me out of my thoughts. "Mark, stop at the poolroom before we get to Margo's house."

I pulled into the poolroom lot. I saw Eugene sitting in his car. I parked next to him. He noticed me and got out of his car and came over and got into mine.

"Hey, did you hear the news about Poppi?" he said.

"No, what happened to Poppi? Did she get busted or something?"

"Naw, Tony. She got killed last night."

"No bullshit! Where'd she get killed at?"

"At her house. Someone shot her in the head."

"Damn! I wonder who did that."

"I bet you that Duck and Slim both had something to do with that," Eugene said. "I wonder if they would try to move on us?"

Tony and I said almost simultaneously, "Hell, no! This is our town. We lay the law down."

"I'm with you all the way no matter what we have to do," Eugene said.

"What happened to her crew?" I asked.

"They all dead too!" Eugene answered.

Then Tony spoke up saying, "Poppi and her crew were weak anyway."

"Tony, didn't you tell me once that Poppi's husband was in Jackson Penitentiary doing life?"

"Yeah, Mark. She was paying his appeal lawyer for him."

"That's fucked up. He's on his own now."

"Yeah, it is."

"Eugene, how's the dope moving?"

"Man, that shit is so good they are going crazy over it. I've got us being millionaires in no time. As soon as I left your house at nine o'clock this morning, when I got back home, Dollar Bill was already there waiting on me."

"I thought that I told everybody last night that you would have their packages at twelve noon?"

"You did, but Dollar Bill felt that I would have the package earlier, so he decided to come by and check. He wanted to get out there and get a jump on everybody."

"Well, Eugene, that's why they call him Dollar Bill. He be after that paper," Tony said.

"What about Tommy, Curtis and Jerome? What time did they pick up their packages?" I asked.

"They all made it somewhere between eleven and eleven thirty, Mark."

"That's good. It shows that they was all anxious to get started. Listen, I was looking for Steve. Have you seen him down here?"

"He hasn't been through since I've been down here. And I've been here for about an hour now."

"Listen, he's supposed to have some guns. If they are new or damn near new, cop them."

"Will do, Tony."

"Okay, we are going to have to go, Eugene. Talk to you later."

Eugene got out of the car and we pulled off headed for Margo's house. On the way, we stopped on the set. As soon as we pulled up and parked, we saw Curtis standing down the street across from the dry cleaners. There were so many people standing around him, it was like he was a celebrity or something. But they were only there to cop.

He didn't notice Tony and me down the block from him. He was busy serving everyone. Tony and I got out of the car. We'd decided to kick it with some of the people for a while and get a feel for how our stuff was moving.

Everybody was coming up to us telling us how good the shit is that Tommy, Curtis and Dollar Bill have. We were walking around talking to a little bit of everybody that Tony knew. Then this elegant young lady walked over to us. She didn't look like someone who did drugs. Tony introduced me to her. Her name was Betty Cobbs.

Tony had known her for a while. We decided that we'd better get moving now. We jumped back into the car and headed once again for Margo's.

Five minutes later, I pulled up down the street from her house and parked. We walked up onto the porch. Tony knocked on the door. Margo answered the door looking as sweet as the first time that I laid eyes on her. She invited us in.

We followed her in. Tony told her that he wanted to show her how to cut and bag up some dope. She led us into the kitchen. There was a kitchen table with a glass top and four chairs around it. We sat down. Tony sat the dope and lactose on the table. Margo went to the drawer and pulled out a set of measuring spoons. I'd forgotten the aluminum foil, so I went back to the car to get it.

When I came back in, Tony was explaining the setup to her saying that Eugene was our lieutenant. He's the one that will be bringing our money and picking up dope as needed. "Your job is to keep enough dope bagged up so that he don't have to wait around," Tony said.

I started mixing the dope with the lactose, sifting the mixture over and over until the whole thing was mixed evenly. Then we showed Margo how to bag it. He brought a pound of heroin and after I cut it, it came out to be six pounds. I then bagged it up. I had 96 ounces of strong street dope. The best in the city, and you can still step on it twice and can't no one touch it. Now that's some good shit!

Tony instructed Margo, "When Eugene comes by, he will leave all of the money with you. You then give him what he needs. If there are any problems, get in touch with Eugene, Mark or myself. No one knows that you are holding, but Eugene, Mark and me. Within a few days, we will have two safehouses, one for the dope and the other for the money. You, Mark and myself will be the only ones that know where these houses are. Now Margo, listen carefully. Whenever you go to one of these houses, always be aware of your surroundings. Make sure that you are not being followed. Always go a different way each time. Any questions before we leave?"

"No, Tony, you've covered everything. Oh, I'm sorry. I do have one question. How much will I make?"

"We'll start you off with twenty-five hundred a week. As we blow up, you blow up."

"Damn! Thanks, Tony, I wasn't expecting to make that much!"

"Baby, we're getting ready to get big as hell. We will be selling to dope dealers in Saginow, Flint and Jackson, Michigan. Even in Ohio."

"Margo, May I use your phone?" I asked.

She handed me the telephone. I called Joyce. The phone just rang and rang. I hung it up.

"Tony, I guess they are still out shopping."

"Brenda must have gotten her mother's car and picked Joyce up."

The doorbell rang. Margo answered it. It was Eugene. He came into the kitchen.

"Man, that shit is moving like hell. Everybody is talking about how good it is. It's all over town. We are going to be some rich brothers!"

I went over and gave him a hug. "That's beautiful, baby, Beautiful."

We talked business for a few minutes, then Eugene left. Tony was standing in the doorway. I looked over at Margo. She saw me staring. "What's wrong?" she asked.

"Nothing, baby, it's just that you look as good today as you did the day that I first met you." She blushed. "I was wondering if I could come by and kick it with you sometime?"

"Sure, Mark, why not?"

I looked into her big brown eyes. "Give me about a week. Tony and I are gonna be busy, but I should have some time in about a week. Cool?"

"I would like that," she smiled, as Tony and I left the house.

Within a week, each person had turned over several times. Money was starting to pour in. Eugene was proving to be the soldier that Tony had predicted he would be. I, myself, was even seeing the qualities in him. He was strong and he was very loyal. And a man's loyalty is very important in this game. Two months had passed and I still hadn't made it over to date Margo. Every time that I went by to pick up money or drop off dope, I would tell her, "Next week."

I'd decided in my mind that Margo and I would remain friends. She was an intelligent, sweet, loyal woman, and I didn't want to mix business with pleasure.

I heard that Slim had left town. The competition was too strong. Word was that he had set up shop in Flint, Michigan. I didn't know how good he was doing and I really didn't care.

Duck was still in business, but barely. He would come around and practically beg Tony and me to sell him some of our dope. He said that he had a few loyal white customers and that it wouldn't interfere with us. Just enough for him to eat and pay a few bills. We discussed it and we agreed to sell him a little. Duck had been known to Tony since Tony was a little child, so Tony looked out for him.

Chapter Five

Summer of 1973...

T he airplane had just landed. Tony and I were just coming into Detroit Metro Airport. We had come from Atlanta, Georgia. We'd just purchased homes for ourselves. I got a nice deal. Eight hundred thousand dollars for a 7,000 square foot, five bedroom mansion. There was a swimming pool, a two-hundred foot drive, a marble foyer, crystal chandeliers, an exercise room and a family room.

It had everything that I could think of. It had a twelve-seat dining table in the huge dining room. It even had quarters for the maids that kept the place beautiful.

We got off the plane, picked up our luggage and walked out of the lobby. My cinnamon gold Cadillac with a cocoa brown top pulled up.

"Hey, baby!" Joyce called out to me.

I waved and walked over to the car. She popped open the trunk and we put our suitcases in it. I walked around and Joyce jumped out and kissed me. Brenda jumped out and kissed Tony.

"Look what I picked up for you, baby!" I pulled a three-carat marquise diamond ring out of my pocket. "This is for you, baby, and this is just the beginning of our life of luxury."

"Oh, my god! It's so big and beautiful!"

I took her hand and placed the sparkling diamond ring on her finger. Tears instantly began rolling down her beautiful face.

"Thank you, baby! I love it!" she said hugging and kissing me. Joyce showed the ring to Brenda.

"Joyce, it's beautiful!" Brenda said admiring the beautiful stone. Tony was standing beside the car. He was staring at Brenda. Brenda was staring back with her hand on her hip.

Tony said, "Come on over here, girl, before I get me another woman." His right hand was behind his back.

Brenda walked over to him, her hand still on her hip. "Quit playing, Tony, you don't need no other woman."

"You know that I love you and would never forget you," Tony said. He pulled his hand from behind his back and handed her a gold bracelet filled with diamonds. Brenda was speechless. She held her arm out for Tony to put the bracelet on her wrist.

"Do you like it, baby?" Tony asked.

"No, baby, I love it!" Brenda said, jumping into Tony's arms, kissing him all over his smiling face. "Thank you, thank you, baby."

"Let's go, everybody," I said as we all got into the Cadillac. "By the way, how do you like this?" I held up my hand showing them my newly purchased five-carat perfectly cut stone.

Tony and I were sitting in the back seat relaxing from the trip from Atlanta. Joyce turned around and looked at the gorgeous ring.

"Oh, baby, that is nice. Look at it Brenda. Isn't it gorgeous?"

Both girls admired the ring. Then they admired each other's gifts. Finally, we headed home.

"Did you have a nice trip?" Brenda asked Tony.

"We sure did, beautiful. It was really a great trip for all of us," Tony said smiling.

"For all of us? What do you mean for all of us?" Brenda was trying to figure out what Tony was talking about.

I decided to spill the beans. "Tony and I are going to send you ladies to Atlanta next week to finish up some business for us."

Tony started laughing.

"Business? What kind of business?" Joyce curiously asked.

Tony and I looked at each other and then I finally told them. "When Tony and I were down in Atlanta, we bought a couple of mansions."

"Mansions! What kind of mansions?" the ladies asked.

"Mine is about 7,000 square foot and Tony's is about 7,000 square foot. And both of you ladies have to go down and furnish them. An interior decorator has already been hired to help out." Both women were surprised and speechless. Tony and I had good women and we wanted them to have all of the best things in life.

When we got back to Lansing, we went to Margo's house to pick up what money she had. She had blown up with us. She was still keeping our stash and Eugene still dropped off money and picked up dope from her. We had several houses set up. Each one of our guys now had people working for them. Duck was struggling bad. He was pretty much broke.

Tony and I had decided to help Duck out. We let him keep his house, but he was now working for us. And he was beginning to blow up all over again.

By now, each of our workers was worth well over a million dollars apiece, depending on whether they spent like crazy or not. We were very organized and none of the crew was using, and they all were loyal. How many organizations can say that?

Everything was running smoothly. Then one hot, humid Tuesday morning, we had just dropped Joyce and Brenda off at the airport headed for Atlanta, Georgia to decorate the houses. We had just pulled up into Tony's driveway. While we were getting out of the car, Eugene pulled up.

"Hey, Eugene," I said as he was walking toward us.

"Hi, Mark, hey, Tony. I'm afraid that I have some bad news."

"What is it, Eugene?" Tony asked.

"Jerome just got arrested. He just called me. He was on his way to my house to drop off and pick up. The police pulled him over before he could make it."

"So what did they get?" Tony asked. "Did they catch him with any dope?"

"No, all they got was the money."

Tony had us all go into the house. He then offered us something to drink to calm the tension.

"Maybe we should call our attorney," I said while sipping on my drink.

"You're right, Mark. Let me go and get my phone book." Tony walked into his bedroom. A few minutes later he returned, phone book in hand. He sat on the couch next to me and flipped through the pages until he located Attorney Williams. He then picked up the phone and dialed the number. "Hello, may I speak to Mr. Jeffery Williams, please? Tell him Anthony Moore is calling."

Attorney Jeffery Williams came to the phone. "Hello, Tony. How are you?"

"I'm fine, Mr. Williams, but I have a problem. One of my guys just got arrested."

"What did they charge him with, Tony?"

"Well, sir, it's my understanding that they only got him on some money."

"Are you sure it's just money?"

"That's my understanding, sir."

"Alright then, Tony. When he goes to court in the morning, I'll take care of everything and you can take care of me later. Give my regards to Mark."

"Will do. Thank you. I'll see you in the morning," Tony said, hanging up the phone.

"He told me to tell you hi, Mark."

"Is everything cool, Tony?"

"Yeah, everything's cool. He'll be out tomorrow."

"Okay, well, that's done. I might as well get out and pick up some money," Eugene said.

"Yeah, man, and I think that I am going home and get some rest since Joyce is gone. I don't have to worry about her pulling on my joint."

"Yeah, you are probably the one pulling on her," Tony said, as we both laughed.

I went on home to get some much needed rest.

The next morning, our attorney met Jerome at court. Jerome was free within the hour. Our attorney called Tony. I was already at Tony's house. We were both waiting to hear what had happened.

"Hello, Tony."

"Hello, Mr. Williams."

"How'd it go?"

"Good, he's on his way to you."

"Okay, I'll send someone down to give you something."

"Tony, they'll drop the charges if you'll forfeit the money."

"Well, forget the money, let them keep it."

"Okay, Tony, I'll handle it."

As soon as he hung up, the doorbell rang. Tony quickly opened the door when he saw that it was Jerome.

"I'm sorry about the money, Tony," Jerome said.

"Things like that happen in this game. Don't worry about the money. We can always make more money," I said.

"That's right, man, what's important is that they didn't catch you with no shit. If they had, it would have been much worse," Tony said.

"Well, I'm just upset about losing so much money. I guess that I'll get out there and try to make it up."

"I'm out of here, too," I said, following Jerome out the door.

I stopped on Logan Street. I had just come out of the store. My car was parked on the street. I was on the passenger side getting ready to walk around the car. Someone blew their horn at me. I waved back at them. I started to walk around my car and I saw this beautiful young lady walking by. I said, "Hello, beautiful. Where are you going?"

She stopped and said, "I'm going to get something to eat."

"Where are you going to get something to eat at?"

"At the rib house on Butler Street."

"I haven't seen you around here before."

"But I've seen you."

"Where have you seen me?"

"I've seen you with Tony many times. And I've seen you at the rib house on Butler Street."

"That's funny that you've noticed me, someone as beautiful as you are, and I never noticed! I can't believe that!"

"Maybe it's because you have so many women."

"That I don't have."

"Are you trying to tell me that you don't have a woman?"

"Now that's not what I'm saying. I'm just saying that I don't have a whole bunch of women. I have a woman with room for one more. Are you with anyone?"

"No, I don't have a man."

"As pretty as you are, you don't have a man?"

"That's right."

"Don't you want a man?"

"If I could find a good one, maybe."

"Well, you are looking at a good one."

"But you said that you are taken."

"I also said that I had room for one more good woman. Are you a good woman?"

"I think that I'm a very good woman if a man is good to me."

"I'd like to be good to you."

"But I don't even know you."

"You know more about me than I know about you. You said that you've been seeing me around. You've been watching me."

"No, I haven't been watching you. I've seen you around, that's what I said."

"Come on, sweetheart, get in the car and let me take you to get something to eat. Have you ever eaten at the Taste of Honey Restaurant downtown on Kalamazoo Street?"

"No, I haven't."

"May I treat you to lunch?"

"Yes, thank you."

She got into the car and I drove over to Kalamazoo Street, parked and we went in. She said that she was hungry and I was too. We sat at a nice table in the middle of the restaurant. Before we ordered, I said, "Baby, we've talked so much, but I haven't even asked you your name and I haven't told you mine. My name is Mark, baby."

"And my name is Joy," she smilingly said.

I asked her what she wanted to order. "You do the ordering," she said.

I was going through the menu as the waitress walked up. "Are you guys ready to order?"

"Yes, we're ready," I said.

"Okay, what would you like to have?"

"Oven baked chicken, mashed potatoes and gravy, green beans, corn on the cob and corn bread."

"What would you guys like to drink?"

I looked at Joy. "What would you like, Joy?"

Coke would be fine, Mark."

"Okay, we'll take two cokes with that. And we'll order dessert after we eat our dinner. If there is any room for dessert."

Joy chuckled.

We enjoyed our lunch and I asked her if she would come with me to the movies this weekend. She said yes. I asked where she lived and she told me at 2436 Washinaw Avenue. I drove her home. We sat in front of her house for a moment. She told me that she enjoyed herself and thanked me for the lunch.

"You're welcome, sweetheart. It was my pleasure." I held her hand and looked into her eyes and said, "I'll see you this weekend," and I left and went home and got me some rest.

Chapter Six

Tony had gone to Philadelphia on business. I was talking to him on the phone.

"Tony, I'm going to have Joyce and Brenda fly back home tomorrow. I'm going into Detroit to pick them up."

"I've already talked to Brenda," Tony Said.

"You know, I still haven't seen that little cutie named Joy that I met."

"You really like her, don't you?"

"Yeah, man, she's really cool. I do like her."

"How's business?" Tony asked.

"Business is great. I've got us a two-building deal waiting when you get back. All of my other businesses are doing fine."

"That's good news, Mark. I'll see you in about two weeks."

"Cool, see you then."

The next morning I was up, showered and out of the house early. I was on my way to Detroit Airport to pick up Joyce and Brenda. As I pulled up, I saw them standing, waiting.

Joyce got into the car. "Hi, baby, did you miss me?"

"Of course I missed you, sweetheart," I said as she kissed me.

Brenda said, "Hi, Mark."

"Hi, Brenda."

"I miss my baby, too. I'll be glad when he comes home next week."

On the way back to Lansing, Joyce and Brenda didn't stop talking. They wanted me to know everything. They described the color of each room. They both used the interior designer that we had hired. Joyce described the master bedroom. She had always wanted a mahogany king sized bed. Now she had one. Her voice was very excited.

Brenda went on and on about her living room. I laughed to myself. I was glad that the two women were pleased. They went on even more about the clothes that they had bought. Their closets in our new homes were half full already. They'd decided not to carry all of those clothes from the mansions in Atlanta all the way back to Lansing.

When we got back, I dropped Brenda off at home then Joyce and I headed home. Later that night, the phone rang. I looked at the clock that sat on the nightstand by the phone. It was 2:15 a.m. I wondered who would be calling me this time of night. The phone rang again. I answered it.

"Hello."

"Hello, Mark, it's me, Eugene."

"What's up, Eugene?"

"We need to talk. It's important. Can you come right now?"

"Where are you, Eugene?"

"I'm at home."

"I'm on my way."

I got out of bed and started getting dressed. Joyce woke up. She glanced at the clock. "Where are you going this early in the morning, baby?"

"Eugene just called and said that it was important that I meet him right now! Maybe one of the houses got busted. I'll be back in an hour." I then kissed Joyce and left.

I pulled the big Caddy into Eugene's driveway. As soon as I walked up to the door, it opened. Eugene stepped back. "Come in, Mark."

"I stepped in. "What's so important, baby, that you got me out of bed?"

"Come into the living room," Eugene said.

I walked into the living room. There sitting on the sofa was Tommy and Dollar Bill.

Eugene stood in front of me. "Look, baby, we have some bad news. Duck is dead. Someone robbed and killed him and his man, Jack."

"Get the fuck out of here! Do y'all know who did it?"

Eugene sat on the sofa next to Dollar Bill. "No, we don't know anything right now."

"The word on the street is that Duck had died immediately and that Jack managed to crawl next door and asked them to call for help. He then died by the time that the ambulance had arrived," Tommy said.

I asked, "Who told you and Dollar Bill about it?"

"It was dope fiend Marvin. He was on his way around there to cop."

"Did you ask him if he saw anybody around there?"

"Yeah, we asked him, but he said that the police and ambulance were there by the time that he got there. Then he asked us for some dope for telling us what little information that he had. We gave him twenty-five dollars and sent him on his way."

"Where is Jerome and Curtis?" I asked.

"They may be at home this time of morning," answered Dollar Bill.

"Tommy, have you talked to him?"

"No, I haven't."

"I want all of you to keep your eyes open and your ears peeled back until we find these mother fuckers that robbed and killed Duck. I want somebody to call Curtis and Jerome and tell them what happened and to be careful. Tighten up security on all of our houses until we find out who did this. Okay, I'm going to get back home to my woman and get me some sleep. Let me know if you find out anything."

After I had driven home, I walked into the bedroom still intoxicated from what I'd heard from Eugene and the fellows. Now I had to break the news to Tony.

Joyce awakened. "Is everything alright? Did one of your houses get busted?"

"No, baby, everything is okay. You can go back to sleep."

I then walked into the living room to call Tony. I dialed Tony in Philly.

Tony answered, still half asleep. "Hello."

"Tony, this is Mark."

"What's up, Mark, what time is it?"

"Somewhere around 3 or 4 o'clock. Tony, this is important. Someone hit and robbed one of our houses. They killed Duck and his man Jack."

Tony was jarred awake. "Killed Duck! Do they know who did it?"

"No. I've got everybody out trying to find out now."

"I'm flying back today."

"No, Tony stay there and finish up with the business. I'll handle everything on this end."

"But I've been knowing that old man since I was a kid."

"I know, Tony, but I've got it. You need to stay focused on that end. By the way, how does it look with the Nigerians?"

"It looks like they're going to be good business partners."

We hung up and I undressed and got into bed. Joyce had fallen back to sleep. Within minutes I was asleep too.

It had been a week since I last talked to Tony and I hadn't heard anything about who killed Duck. I was beginning to think that it was somebody from out of town. Then we got a line on something. There was this lady that knows Curtis' woman who said that these three men that are friends of her old man were doing dirtball bad a week ago. Now they have plenty of money and dope and they come by her house and get high with her old man. Curtis' woman asked her friend what they did and asked if they robbed a bank or something. One of them said, "You heard that nigger say, 'Don't do it! Don't do it!' and I silenced his ass." Curtis' woman asked her girlfriend if she knew their names.

She said, "No, but I think one of them was called Big John."

"Big John, huh, thanks."

After Curtis passed this information on to me, I immediately told him to call Big Earl and for him and Big Earl to take care of these mother fuckers.

"Consider it done," Curtis said.

"Let me know when it's all taken care of." I then went on home.

The next day I decided to see Joy. I put on a two-toned Italian knit shirt and a pair of dark brown royal silk pants with a pair of brown gators. I got into my cinnamon gold 1973 Cadillac.

As I was riding to her house, I was thinking that the new 1974s would be out in another month and it would be time for me to get one.

I proceeded on over to her house. As I pulled up in front of her house, Joy happened to be coming out the door. She walked over to my car.

"Hi, baby, how are you doing?" I said.

"I'm fine. How come you haven't been by to see me?"

"Sweetheart, I wanted to, but I've been awfully busy." I liked this girl. I liked her character. Even though I'd disappointed her several times, she always remained sweet. I know that this was someone that I wanted to spend more time with. I wondered what was going through Joy's mind. I know what was going through mine. I wanted this woman to be mine. I love my Joyce, but I feel a need to have Joy as well.

Joy was thinking to herself at the same time. I like Mark. He's very attractive. And so sweet. He always says the right thing. He's the type of man that can bring out the romance that lies deep down inside of me.

"Joy, what are you thinking about? You seem like you are in deep thought."

"Oh, I was just thinking about what you are going to ask me next."

"I was going to ask you if you'd like to go out to dinner and maybe to a club later."

"What club do you want to go to?"

"Well, baby, I like several clubs. We could go to the Plush or the Black and Tan Lounge or the Taste of Honey, it's up to you, sweetheart."

"I like the Taste of Honey, myself."

"Then the Taste of Honey it is, baby. Well, get in, sweetheart. Let's go!"

Joy got into the car. I asked her if she liked seafood? She said yes.

"Have you ever been to Bill's Crabhouse and Bar?"

"No, but I've heard that it was really nice there. I hear that they have a nice jazz band next door at the Taste of Honey."

"What do you know about jazz, and you are only eighteen years old?"

"I like Grover Washington, Miles Davis, John Coltrain, Nancy Wilson and many more," she said.

On our way to the crabhouse, we went down Chestnut Street. We passed the Cocoa Lounge.

I asked her, "Do you see the Cocoa Lounge over there?"

She said yes.

"Well, I own it."

"Really? You own the Cocoa Lounge? I've been in there a few times. It's a really nice place inside."

"Thank you, I renovated the whole place after I bought it."

We parked and went into the restaurant. Before we could order, Joy went to the restroom. I watched her as she walked away. I heard someone say, "Damn, look at that." I looked over my right shoulder to see who it was. I saw two guys sitting at the table behind me staring at Joy with their mouths open.

I looked to see what they were looking at and I saw this perfectly formed body of this goddess that was already in my presence. It was as if I'd seen Joy for the very first time. She was wearing a miniskirt. I've always seen her in pants with her chocolate complexion.

Now I have two beautiful women. One is light complected with big brown eyes and a beautiful shape. The other is chocolate. One is Joyce and the other is Joy. How lucky can a man be?

Joy returned from the restroom.

I asked Joy, "What do you want to eat?"

"I'll have a seafood platter?"

"I'll have the same."

The waitress approached the table. "Are you ready to place your order?"

"Yes, we'd like to get two seafood platters and a couple of cokes. Can we get a large order of crab legs right now for an appetizer?"

"Will that be all, sir?"

"Yes, thank you."

"Excuse me, excuse me, ma'am. Could you tell me what time the live jazz starts next door at the Taste of Honey?"

"It starts at 8 o'clock."

"Thank you."

"You are welcome."

I asked Joy, "Do you have any brothers or sisters?"

"Yes," she answered. "I have a brother named Michael and a sister named Diane. I'd like for you to meet my whole family. My mother and my father too."

"I ain't too good with old ladies and old men."

"My mother and father are not old."

"Baby, I didn't mean it that way. It was just a figure of speech."

"I know you didn't mean it that way. I was just kidding with you."

"So what are we going to do, hang out all night?"

"It's cool with me," she said.

We ate, had a nice dinner, then went next door to the jazz club and had a lovely time together.

"Joy, you know that most people your age don't like jazz."

"What about your age?"

"Baby, I'm twenty-three."

"Mark, you ain't nothing but five years older than me. I'm eighteen."

"You're right, baby. I remember that I liked jazz at eighteen too. I've always been in love with Nancy Wilson."

"Do you like Al Green?"

"Yes, I like Al Green. Lay Your Head Upon My Pillow. I really like that song."

"I really like it, too. I've got it at home."

"What was that last performer's name, baby?"

"His name was Pharaoh Sanders."

"He sounded just like John Coltrain."

"Well, baby, I think that it is time to go. Drink you drink, baby, for we can get up out of here."

In the car I asked her, "Joy, would you like to stay with me tonight or would you want to go home?"

She looked me in my eyes and said, "I want to stay with you."

At that moment, I leaned over. We embraced and we kissed. I then drove over to the Motel 6 on Michigan Avenue.

Inside the suite...

First we disrobed. As she stood before me with her Hershey chocolate complexion, her body was smooth as silk. Not a blemish anywhere. Her breasts stood at attention. I motioned for her to come to me. We were both naked. I put my hand on her shoulders. I leaned over and sucked on her neck. I ran my tongue up her neck to her chin, then back down to her nipple. I licked in a wide circle on her body. I licked one nipple then the other. I licked my way down her body. When I got down to her thighs, I put my hand on her leg and lifted it up onto the bed.

I kissed her hairy bush. She shivered with anticipation of more. She started moaning and groaning and pulling my head in closer.

I slowly lay her back on the bed. I spread her legs wide as I ate her pussy. I licked and sucked. She started to shake all over. I continued to lick her sweet juicy pussy. I slowly slipped my finger into her ass as I ate her even more. I kissed my way back up her body. I took her finger and placed it into my mouth. I sucked on her finger for a moment. I pushed her all the way flat on the bed. I eased my way up her body until my dick was level with her head. I turned her head toward me and eased my dick into her warm, wet mouth.

She sucked on my dick, then pulled my dick out of her mouth, running her tongue up and down the length of my shaft.

She would take my balls into her mouth and suck on them too. She sucked on me like she was hungry.

I lay her back and spread both legs wide. I eased my dick into her pussy. She grabbed my ass and pulled me all the way into her wet, hot pussy. We fucked like that for a while. Then we changed positions with her on top. She rode me and rode me. She started calling my name over and over. "Oh, Mark, Mark, Mark." After she came again, I started fucking her from behind. Finally, I came. I came hard.

We both lay in each other's arms. She kissed me on the neck. I looked over at my beautiful Joy. She was everything that I had hoped for and more. Se was my Joy. As the sunlight shined through the window, I got up and closed the curtain. I lay back down and we both dozed off to sleep.

That afternoon, Joy and I enjoyed another round of lovemaking before I drove her home. Once she was safe inside, I drove home as well.

Chapter Seven

Later that night, Eugene called and said that he had something important to talk to me about. I told him to come on over to my house so that we could talk.

Fifteen minutes later, there was a knock on the door. I opened it. It was Eugene.

"Come on in, Eugene." We walked to the living room. I told him to have a seat and offered him a drink.

"No, thank you, Mark. I have something that we need to talk about."

"Okay, what is it?"

Eugene then glanced toward Joyce.

I said, "Excuse us for a minute, baby. We need to talk."

Eugene said, "Curtis called and he and Big Earl found out where those assholes that killed old man Duck was holed up. They are at Darlene Fisher's house on Walnut Street getting high. Dope fiend Marvin told them where they were. They said that they were ready to make a move on them tonight."

I said, "Cool. Make sure that they tell them that it's from old man Duck."

I was thinking to myself, I needed to call Tony and let him know what was happening. He's still in Philadelphia taking care of business with the Nigerians. I decided that this would be a good time to call. "Excuse me, Eugene, for a minute." Then I got up and walked out of the room. I sat down on my bed and dialed Tony's number in Philly. The phone rang and kept ringing. I was just about to hang up when I heard a voice say, "Hello."

"Tony, this is Mark."

"Mark, what's happening, baby?"

"Man, I've got some good news."

"What's that, baby?"

"Eugene is here now. He just ran down to me that Curtis and Big Earl have located the three assholes that did Duck. Dope fiend Marvin gave them the line on them. They are going to make their move tonight."

"Sounds good, Mark. Sounds real good. I like hearing good news like that."

"Man, I was about to hang up the phone, it took so long for you to answer."

"I was in the shower, Mark."

"So dig, when are you coming back?"

"I'll be there tomorrow, Mark."

"I'm done on this end. We are good to go. Tony, you know that your woman Brenda is missing the hell out of you. She and Joyce have been hanging together every day."

"I know. I miss her too."

"So tell me, Tony, have you guys ever been away from each other this long before?"

"Not this long, Mark, maybe a week. I went to St. Louis when my mother's mother was sick, but that's about it. And that was the only time."

"Does Brenda know that you are coming in tomorrow?"

"No, I'm going to call her and let her know."

"Have you talked to your mother, Tony?"

"Yeah, every other day. She's cool."

"I saw your little sister the other day, Tony, and I gave her some money to go shopping with."

"Thanks, Mark, that girl loves to shop."

"Yeah, man. Well, I'm going to let you go. Hopefully everything will be taken care of before you arrive."

"Alright, Mark, I'll talk to you."

"Yeah, later, Tony." After we hung up I walked back into the living room.

"Sorry it took so long, Eugene, I was on the phone with Tony."

"How is Tony? When will he be back?"

"He's cool. He'll be back soon."

"Okay, Mark, I'm going to leave now."

"Let me know when it's over."

After Eugene left, I went back into the bedroom where Joyce was sitting on the bed watching TV. I joined her.

At that same time...

Curtis and Big Earl were creeping around to the back of Darlene Fisher's house. Curtis had drawn his .357 and Big Earl had his two 45's drawn. One in each hand. The yard was very dark. They peeked in the window. They saw the four of them sitting at the table. Curtis signaled to Big Earl to remain quiet. Curtis knocked on the door.

"Who is it?" Darlene asked.

Curtis disguised his voice. "It's Marvin."

"Hold up, Marvin, here I come."

As soon as the door opened, Big Earl and Curtis rushed in knocking Darlene to the floor. Big Earl moved with surprising quickness. The three men sitting at the table suddenly were jarred out of their nods.

Curtis hit the first man that he came to with the butt of his gun. Big Earl stuck the barrel of his 45 into one of the men's mouth.

"Damn," shouted Big Earl, "I think this one just shit his pants."

Curtis stood in front of them so that he could see all of their hands. "Nobody move until I say so."

Darlene was trembling. Some of the men trembled more than she did. Big Earl closed the door, making sure that no one had seen them. Curtis ordered everybody to get up and go down to the basement. Everyone marched into the basement.

"On your knees," Big Earl ordered.

Curtis stepped up. "This is for old man Duck."

"Old man Duck! I didn't have nothing to do with that," screamed Darlene.

"Me neither," cried Joseph. "It was him. It was Big John that killed him." He pointed to the heaviest of the three men. Big Earl walked over to the big man and said, "Do you believe in God?"

Big John agreeably nodded his head.

"Good, then say your prayers."

Both men opened fire. All three guns blazing away. The four bodies bounced and jerked across the floor.

When all of the guns were empty, the men stopped. Blood poured out from under the bodies. Big John's arm moved. Big Earl reloaded one of his 45's and walked over to the dying man. "For Duck." Then he put the gun to the back of John's head and pulled the trigger. Blood splattered onto the bottom of his pants. John's brain lay in front of Big Earl's feet.

Curtis motioned to Earl and they left. They went back to Curtis' house and cleaned up. Then they called Eugene and said, "It's over, it's done."

"That's music to my ears. I'll let Mark know." Eugene then hung up and called Mark.

"Hello," I answered.

"Mark, this is Eugene. Everything is everything."

"Alright, Eugene, good night." I hung up the phone, hugged Joyce and went back to sleep.

Chapter Eight

I woke up the next morning and went into the shower. Joyce was in the kitchen cooking breakfast. She'd already showered and dressed. She was cooking my favorite breakfast—pancakes, eggs with cheese, and grits with beef sausage, sided with a tall, cold glass of orange juice. I could smell the sausage cooking as I was getting dressed.

I was really hungry that morning. I had a big appetite. Maybe it was because we had avenged Duck's death. I don't know. But I really enjoyed my breakfast.

As I was finishing my meal, Joyce had just gotten off the phone with Brenda. She was ready, waiting for us to come and pick her up. I wiped my mouth with my napkin and put the dishes into the sink.

"Let's go, baby," I said.

Fifteen minutes later we were in front of Brenda's house. I blew my horn and she came out and got into the car. "Hi, Joyce. Hi, Mark. I'm so excited. My baby is coming home today. He has never been away from me this long. Next time you are gonna have to go, Mark."

"Girl, don't be trying to send my man away," said Joyce.

They both started laughing. Brenda and Joyce had become very good friends. As had Tony and I.

On the way to the airport, the two girls kept up a steady conversation, but my mind had wandered off to Joy and the wonderful time that we had together. I loved Joyce with all of my heart, but there was room in the temple of my heart for Joy. We parked in front of the airport. Brenda got out to go and get Tony. A few moments later, they came out to the car. I popped the trunk and helped Tony put his suitcases into it.

I gave Tony a hug and said, "It's good to have you back."

"It's good to be back, baby," he said.

I drove Tony and Brenda home. I helped Tony with the suitcases. I hugged Tony again and whispered into his ear, "It's done. We've avenged Duck's death."

"Good man, I'm glad that's done. Look man, I need to spend some time with my woman. I'll call you in a couple of days. I'll fill you in on the Nigerians."

"Cool. I'll talk to you then."

"Cool," Tony said, walking away.

I then drove home.

I was getting dressed when I heard the doorbell ring.

"Baby, could you get that?"

"Yes, sweetheart."

"Thank you, baby."

Joyce opened the door. "Hi, Tony."

Tony answered, "Hi, Joyce. Is Mark in?"

"Yes, he's in. Come on in, Tony, and have a seat. He's getting dressed. Would you like something to drink?"

"No, thank you, Joyce."

"Let me see if he's dressed."

"Thank you, Joyce."

I came out of the bedroom and into the living room where Tony was sitting. "What's up, baby? Good to see you."

He smiled and said, "It's good to see you too, Mark."

"I was beginning to think that Brenda wasn't going to let you out." We both laughed.

Then Tony said, "Let me run down to you, baby, what transpired in Philly. All about our people, Solako and Kamara, the Nigerians. We had a lot to talk about. They want us to do business with them, with diamonds. There is a lot of money to be made. They will sell them to us below wholesale price, whereas we can sell to jewelers at wholesale price. They guarantee the quality of these diamonds are strictly the best. Now Mark, I like this idea of dealing diamonds, because there is a passion for them. I want us to set up a company in Atlanta."

"Excuse me, Tony, what are we talking about as far as capital?" I asked.

"We can start with as little as $150,000. But I was thinking that we would start with $250,000. How does that sound to you, Mark?"

"It sounds good, Tony."

"I told them that I would let them know within a week, after I ran it down to you. I said that I don't do anything without my partner agreeing to it." Mark smiled. "I am optimistic, Mark, that this thing can work. What do you think?"

"I realize, Tony, that one day we will have to get out of this drug game. And planning for the future is a good thing. We need to go all of the way legit."

"You are right, and we are on our way," Tony said.

"Then, Tony, I'm for it. We both have lots of money to work with. We've both purchased apartment buildings, beautiful mansions in Atlanta, and we have our hands in a few other things as well. I am always looking for business opportunities, Tony. We have done well together. Why stop now?"

"I feel the same."

"Listen, Tony, all I'm asking is, let's just put this on hold for about a month until we move into our mansions in Atlanta."

"I have no problem with that, Mark. I'll call them and let them know that it will be longer than a week."

"Good. By the way, Nigeria is known for its oil, isn't it?"

"Yes, but Solako and Kamara get their diamonds from Sierra Leone."

"Oh, I see. Okay. Listen, Tony, since you haven't seen Margo in a while, let's go by and check her out."

"Sounds good to me. Let's go."

"Hold up, Tony." Joyce walked into the living room from the kitchen. "Tony and I are getting ready to make a run. I'll be back in a couple of hours."

"Baby, can you stop at the store on the way home and pick up some milk and some juice?"

"Alright, baby." I kissed Joyce and Tony and I left in his money green 1974 Eldorado. On the way to Margo's, we decided to stop at Eugene's. As we were pulling up, Curtis was coming out of the house. He approached the car.

"How long have you been back, Tony?"

"Oh, I've been back for a few days now, Curtis. Mark told me that you and Big Earl took care of that problem for us."

"Yeah, they all were crying like little bitches. One even shit on himself! We hated to do the broad, but she had to go because she was there."

"Oh, yeah, Curtis, come on back into the house with us. We need to talk to you and Eugene."

We knocked on the door.

"Who is it?"

"Tony and Mark."

"Hold up, baby, here I come." Eugene opened the door. Tony, Curtis and I walked in.

"Tony, what's up, man? It's good to see you."

"Hey, Eugene."

"I was wondering when you were going to make it around to see me."

"I had to spend some time with my woman first. I'd been gone so long."

"Listen, man, Mark and I want to have a talk with you and Curtis. We are getting ready to relocate. We will be leaving in about a week or two. Eugene, you will keep running everything here. Curtis will be your lieutenant."

Curtis smiled.

"Eugene, you will report to Mark and me like always. We will give you the numbers. You will pick up your supplies from our connections lieutenant. We will set all of that up before we leave. Once a month Mark and I will pick up the money or we will send someone to pick it up. Any questions, Eugene?"

"No, I'm cool with it."

"What about you, Curtis?"

"I'm cool with it as well."

"Alright. Everybody else will keep doing what they've been doing. My girl, Margo, she will keep holding for us. I guess that's it, unless you have something to add, Mark?"

"No, Tony, I think you've covered just about everything."

Eugene said, "Bet you can't guess who I saw yesterday, Tony?"

"Who?"

"Slim."

"He's back in town?"

"Yeah, and he's really looking bad."

"He should be. We ran him out of business, what do you expect?" I said. They all started laughing.

"He's not the only one that we ran out of business," Curtis said.

Tony said, "Alright fellows. If there's nothing else, Mark and I are out of here."

Both men said that's it. Tony and I left heading over to Margo's.

Tony said, "Me and that girl have been cool for over twelve years. I remember in school, all of the boys used to tease her about her bowlegs. Now that we're grown, all of the boys are trying to get between those bowlegs. She's always been like a little sister to me. I remember getting into a couple of fights over her in school."

"Tony, I can see the closeness between the two of you. She's gong to be really glad to see you. She asks me about you every time that I see her."

"Yeah, that's my girl, Mark."

As we pulled in front of the house, I said, "Tony, you know we have come a long ways, baby."

"Yeah, Mark, but the road is long and we still have a ways to go."

"I know. I was just saying, Tony, it feels good. It feels real good."

"I know, baby, I know."

We got out of the car and went into Margo's house. She was so glad to see Tony, she leapt into his arms with her legs wrapped around his waist with a gleam of happiness and joy in her eyes. She gave him a big kiss on the cheek, saying, "Tony, I missed you. I asked Mark about you so much I know he was getting tired of me asking."

"No, I wasn't, Margo. I know how close you and Tony are," I said.

"I missed you too, Margo," Tony said.

"How's Brenda?" Margo asked. "I know that she was going crazy while you were gone."

"She's cool now. I've been back for three days and this is my first day out."

"Tony, tell her that I said hi."

"I will, baby."

"Oh, I'm sorry, Mark. How are you doing, baby?"

"I'm good, Margo. I was beginning to think I was the invisible man here. And I still feel a little bit left out. Where's my kiss?"

Margo put her arms around Mark's neck and kissed him on the cheek and said, "Sweety, you are never left out. I love you too."

"Margo, we stopped by because we wanted to let you know that we are both moving to Atlanta in a week or two. But everything is going to stay the same. You will keep holding for us and deal only with Eugene. If you need anything, one of us will call you, me, or Tony once a week. Is that cool?"

She said, "Yes."

"Baby, we hate to rush, but we've got to make a couple more stops. But we'll see you before we leave."

"Damn, I'm going to miss you all," Margo said.

"Maybe one day when we get our company up and running, we will send for you to come down for a while."

"Would you? I'd love that. I've never been to Atlanta. They say that it is the chocolate city because so many blacks live there. I've heard so much about the underground. Maybe we could go there?"

"I don't see why not, Margo. Wherever you'd like to go, we'll take you. You are our girl. Well, baby, we'd better be going," Tony said.

We walked out and got into the car. As Tony pulled away from the curb, I glanced back and saw Margo standing at the window. She waved goodbye. I thought to myself, she looked so sad as if she'd lost her two friends forever. I turned to Tony and said, "You know, maybe we'll bring Margo down after we are there for a couple of weeks."

"Why so soon, Mark? We told her that once we get our company up and running that we would send for her for a while."

"I know what we said, but as you were pulling off from the curb, I saw the sadness in her eyes that I'd never seen before. It was as if she was losing the only two friends that she had. I really dig her, and I too love her like a sister now. So what do you say?"

"It's cool with me, Mark, it's cool with me."

Mark slumped back in his seat and said, "Okay, then, we'll do it."

Tony dropped me off at home. I spent the rest of the evening with Joyce watching movies. We laughed and talked about when times weren't so good, and how far we have come. "Yes, baby, I remember when we first came to Lansing. I was Jonesing and wanted to get off of that shit. I remember the first night that we met Tony. And he took me to find something."

"Yeah, Mark, who would have known that you and Tony would turn out to be best friends?"

"Yeah, baby, that's my man. We've made lots of money together and making big moves. We are two rich young brothers. Still in our twenties. Life has really been good to us. We have truly been blessed."

We talked for about a half an hour more, then we turned off the lights and went to sleep.

Chapter Nine

Two days later...

I decided to go see Joy. I liked the sound of her name, every time I say it. As I turned the corner, I could see Joy's house. Joy and her mother were at the trunk of the car removing groceries. I pulled to the curb and parked. Then got out of the car to help. "Hi, beautiful. Let me help you with that," I politely said. "Hello, Mrs. Reed."

Joy's mother was a beautiful dark-skinned woman with a very shapely body. Joy and her mother looked just alike. Many people mistook them for sisters because her mother was so youthful looking.

Once we had carried all of the groceries into the house, I told Joy that I needed to talk to her. She said that we could go to her room. We walked up the stairs to her room and sat on the bed.

"How's my beautiful black queen been?"

She blushed and said, "I'm fine."

"Baby, you know that I am moving to Atlanta in a couple of weeks."

"Mark, I know that you and Tony bought mansions there. Will I be able to go with you?"

"I will send for you soon. But first, Tony and I are going to set up a new company."

"What kind of company are you and Tony going to set up, honey?"

"It's going to be a diamond company. We are going to sell diamonds to jewelry stores at wholesale prices."

"Do you and Tony have a name for your company yet?"

"No, we really haven't discussed a name yet. But I have one in mind."

"What name do you have in mind, sweetheart?" Joy asked.

"I was thinking about Diamonds Unlimted, Inc., but I need to run that past Tony first to see what he thinks."

"It sounds like a good name to me."

"Yeah, we'll see."

"Baby, you promise that you are going to send for me?"

"Joy, there is no way that I am going to leave you here. You are a part of my life now that I can't do without."

"Mark, until I met you, I wasn't sure if I wanted to be in a relationship again. I never told you this before, but the last man that I was with wasn't shit," she angrily said. "Excuse me, baby, I'm sorry for using such language, but it's the truth. He was very rude and he also beat me a couple of times. I knew that it was time to get out of that relationship and I got out fast. I said that was it for me. And then you came along. I still remember the first day on Logan Street when I was coming out of the store and we started talking. I saw this warmth and compassion in your eyes. I knew you were different. You were such a gentleman."

I looked deep into Joy's eyes. It was as if I went into her soul. I felt the love she had for me. She was the second woman in my life that I felt so close to. Joyce was my first. I have had many women, but none could compare to these two. Am I blessed or what? Two good women and millions of dollars. What a life!

I told my baby that it was time for me to go and that I would be busy for the next couple of days. Then Joy walked me back down the stairs and out to my car. We hugged and kissed and said good bye. I got into my car and drove off.

On my way home, I decided to stop at Joyce and my favorite restaurant, Calhoun's. It was a small place. This really nice black guy owned it. He sold some really good porkchop sandwiches with mayonnaise and hot sauce. I ordered four to go. I stood around for ten or fifteen minutes, small talking. I enjoyed talking to him. He was very friendly and he was a wise old man. Then I said, "Well, Mr. Charles, I think I'd better be running on before these sandwiches get cold. My girl is going to really like what I have in this bag. But she will probably smell them before she sees them."

I left and went straight home. I pulled into my driveway, parked and shut off my car. When I entered the house, Joyce was sitting in the living room watching TV.

"I stopped on the way home and got us..."

Joyce interrupted. "I know, you stopped by Calhoun's, didn't you, baby? You bought us some porkchop sandwiches, didn't you?"

"Naw, baby, I didn't stop by Calhoun's."

"Yes, you did, baby, I could smell the porkchop sandwiches in the bag. Quit playing." She got up and playfully tried to take the bag from my hand. I switched the bag from hand to hand. I wrapped my arms around her and asked her, "Which one do you want, me or the bag?"

She answered, "Baby, you know that I love you, but I want my porkchop sandwich too."

We both laughed. The rest of the day I spent with Joyce. We laughed and had so much fun. I enjoyed spending time with my Joyce. Tony and I had been so busy lately that I hadn't been able to spend much time with Joyce. Today she had my undivided attention. She'd been with me through hell and back. I've always been able to depend on her. She never wavered when times were hard. Every man needs a strong woman like Joyce in their corner. Of course, like anyone else, we have our ups and downs. That's the way life is.

As the day ended and darkness crept up on us, we were still laying on the couch when Joyce said to me, "You know, Mark, I haven't been out on Butler Street for almost a year now."

"Sweetheart, you haven't missed anything. I was just there a couple of weeks ago. You and Brenda spend so much time going to shopping malls in Lansing and Detroit, spending Tony and my money."

"Oh, so now it's Tony and your money? What happened to your and my money?"

"I'm sorry, baby, you know that I was only joking."

"I'll tell you what. Why don't you and I take a ride down on Butler Street?"

"Yeah, baby, let's do that."

"Can we go now?"

"Sure, baby, why not?"

We got up and I felt my pocket. I said, "Where are my keys? I looked on the coffee table. They weren't there. I looked on the end tables and they weren't there either. Joyce reached down between the cushions of the couch and found my keys. We headed out the door, got into the car and proceeded toward Butler Street.

Once we were on Butler Street, I parked my car. Frank and Karen walked over and leaned down. I let down the passenger side window. Frank leaned in and said, "What's up, Mark?"

"Hey, Frank, how are you doing?"

Karen said, "Hi, Mark. Hi, Joyce." We both returned the 'hi' back to Karen.

Joyce said, "It sure is a lot of people out here tonight."

"Girl, it's like this out here every night. These black folks come out like roaches do when you turn out the lights," Karen said.

I said, "Baby, do you want to get out of the car and walk around for a moment?"

"No, baby, I just want to sit in the car and watch. It's like a show to me. I haven't been out here in a while."

"Cool, then, we'll sit here. Hold up. I'm gonna go in and get a couple of pops to drink. I'll be right back."

Joyce asked, "Karen, do you and Frank want to sit down in the car?"

"No, thank you, baby. We were getting ready to leave when we saw y'all pull up. I just wanted to holler at you. I haven't seen you in a while."

"Okay, Karen, you take care."

"Okay, Joyce, you do the same. Bye."

"Baby."

As I was coming out of the bar-b-que joint with the two pops in my hands, I ran into Slim. He was with some guy that I'd never seen before. Slim said, "Mark, my man, how are you?" He extended his hand. I shook it. He said, "Mark, this is my friend, Joe. He's from Flint, Michigan."

I said, "Hello, Joe. Pleased to meet you."

Betty was standing there, wanting to say something to me at the time. Betty is a friend of mine that is getting ready to graduate from law school.

Three years ago, when Betty's father passed away, her mother was about to lose the house because they didn't have any insurance. Betty came to me one day crying. After running her problem down to me, she asked if I could help. I gave her and her mother $15,000. She said that she would repay me one day. I told her that she didn't owe me anything.

"So, Slim, what have you been doing with yourself?"

"Just trying to make a little money, Mark. Just trying to make a little money. Listen, I have a hundred dollars that I owe Tommy. Can you give it to him for me?"

Slim went into his pocket and pulled out a hundred dollars and gave it to me.

I said, "Alright. I'll see that he gets it."

Slim said, "Thank you," and he and his friend left.

I turned to Betty and said, "How have you been, baby?"

"I'm fine, Mark, I'm getting ready to graduate," she said.

I said, "Girl, I'm so proud of you."

"But Mark, it couldn't have happened if you hadn't helped me and my mom out three years ago."

"I am just happy that I was able to help out. So, Betty, how is your mom doing?"

"She's fine, Mark, she really is. She always talks about you."

"Tell her that I said hello. Is there anything else that I can do for you?"

"You are so sweet, Mark. No, we are fine. I just wish that I could do something for you. Well, I've got to go, Mark."

"Okay, I'll see you, baby."

"Bye, Mark." Then she walked away. Betty was a tall, elegant, beautiful young lady with hazel eyes. Her hair draped her shoulders. She walked with confidence. I always saw the potential in her.

I went back to my car and got in. I said to Joyce, "Are you enjoying the show?"

"I sure am. It is like a circus out here."

"Well, baby, what do you want to do now?" I asked.

Joyce took a sip of her pop and said, "We can go home now."

I started the engine and turned on the radio. The O'Jays were on, singing It's a Family Reunion. Joyce looked at me and smiled. "You love that song, don't you, baby?"

I smiled back and said, "Yeah, I really dig that song. That and the Commodores' song, Just To Be Close To You because you mean so much to me."

Joyce leaned over and kissed me on the cheek as I pulled away from the curb. We went on home, got undressed and went to bed. We talked for a while, then drifted off to sleep embraced in each other's arms.

The next morning I woke up. I felt around the bed. Joyce was already up. I called for her and she came into the bedroom. She said, "Yes, baby, what do you need?"

I stretched and yawned. "What are you doing, baby?"

Joyce answered, "I was sitting in the living room drinking some orange juice. Do you want something?"

"Yes, can you make some breakfast for me, baby?"

"What would you like, sweetheart?"

"Fix me some pancakes, scrambled eggs, grits with cheese, hot croissants and butter. I'm going to jump in the shower and then get dressed. Let me know when it's ready."

Once I got out of the shower and got dressed, Joyce called me into the kitchen to eat while the food was still hot. While sitting at the table, I picked up an *Ebony* magazine, which I started reading. Joyce got up and turned on the TV. To my amazement, this prosecutor was on TV talking about a major drug bust that had occurred only last night.

The prosecutor vowed to rid the city of all drugs. He said that there are bigger fish out there and they know who the are. "We will get you!" he said.

I looked at Joyce and said, "Did you hear that shit? I wonder who in the hell they busted last night?" I called Eugene and asked him how our houses were.

"Everything is okay, Mark. Why, is something wrong?"

"I was watching the news and Prosecutor Roland Hindenberg was his name, talking about a major drug bust they made last night."

"It's not us, because Dollar Bill and Tommy had left here an hour ago. And I just hung up from talking to Curtis a few minutes before you called."

"Thanks, Eugene, I'll talk to you later. Y'all be careful," and I hung up. Then I dialed Tony.

"Tony, did you see the news this morning?"

"No, Mark, I haven't had a chance to watch it. What's up?"

"They had this prosecutor saying that they made a decent bust last night."

"Who did they get? Do you know?"

"If they mentioned it, I didn't catch that part. All I know is that this prosecutor sounds like a real asshole. Talking about he's not done yet. He's going to clean up the whole town."

"I'm going to call Eugene and tell him to keep his eyes open and to be careful."

"No, baby, I already ran it down to Eugene. Listen, Tony, I'll see you in a few days. I'm going to spend some time home with Joyce. If you need me, I'll be here."

"Hey, me and Brenda were thinking about going out later on. Would you and Joyce like to go?"

"Where do you plan on going?"

"We were thinking about going to the Black and Tan bar on Grande River."

"Hold on, Tony. Joyce, do you want to go out tonight with Brenda and Tony?"

"Not really, baby. I was hoping that me and you could spend some quality time together."

"Sorry, Tony, I think I'm going to pass this time."

"Alright, baby." With that, we both hung up.

The next few days, I worked around the house helping Joyce do a little bit of everything. It felt good to be out of the streets for a while.

Chapter Ten

I had been at home the whole weekend with Joyce. It was now Monday. For three days I had been in the house, helping my woman and enjoying her company. The phone rang. I answered.

"Hello, may I speak to Mark?"

"Speaking."

"Mark, this is Mr. Goodman."

"Oh, hello, Mr. Goodman." It was my attorney.

"I was wondering if you and Tony could come down to the office right away?"

"Is there something wrong, Mr. Goodman?"

"I can't talk on the telephone. All I can tell you is that it is important that I see you both, right away. You really need to get here fast. Bring Tony with you."

"We'll be there by noon."

"Fine, I'll see you both then."

I hung up the phone. I was caught off guard and confused. I called Tony right away. The phone rang.

Tony answered. "Hello."

"Hey, baby, this is Mark."

"What's up, Mark?"

"Tony, Mr. Goodman just called me. He said that he needed to see the both of us right away. I asked him what it was all about and he said that he didn't want to talk on the phone. This shit sounds serious."

"Yeah, Mark, it sure does."

"Well, let's go down and see what is so important that he couldn't tell us on the phone."

"Tony, I'm on my way to pick you up."

"Cool, Mark. I'll be waiting."

We both hung up and twenty minutes later I was pulling up in Tony's driveway. I blew my horn and Tony came out of the house and got into the car. He looked at me as confused as I was, saying, "I wonder what the hell is going on, Mark?"

"Hell, me too."

We headed to see our attorney. Once we parked, we got out of the car and went into the Government One building where our lawyer's office was located. We took the elevator to the ninth floor. We walked down this long corridor to office 924.

Over the door it read "Goodman and Goldstein and Associates." We opened the door and walked in. We stopped at the receptionist's desk and asked if Mr. Goodman was in.

The young blonde headed woman said, "Who shall I say is here?"

"Tell him it's Mark Jones and Tony Moore."

"One minute, please."

"Thank you."

She picked up the phone and spoke into the receiver. "Mr. Goodman, there is a Mr. Jones and Mr. Moore here to see you."

"Send them in, please."

"Yes, sir. Mr. Goodman will see you now. Go down the hall, the third office on the right is his office."

Tony and I walked down to Mr. Goodman's office. He was sitting behind a big oak desk. He was a big man, about fifty-seven or fifty-eight years old. His brown hair had touches of grey on the side.

"Good afternoon, Mr. Goodman," I said.

"Good afternoon, Mark and Tony." He stood up and shook our hands and said, "Have a seat."

Tony asked, "What's so important that we had to get down here right away, Mr. Goodman?"

Mr. Goodman put his hand on his chin. He looked the both of us in our eyes and asked, "Do either of you know a Raymond Little? They call him 'Slim.'"

Tony said, "Yeah, we both know him. What's up?"

"Well, he's a problem for the both of you."

"How can he be a problem for us?" Tony asked.

"Well, it seems that he's been doing a lot of talking to the narcotics squad. He's their informant. Mark, yours and Tony's names have been coming up. Both of you are under investigation for running a heroin ring. I have someone in the prosecutor's office that I can work with."

"What type of evidence do they have on us?" I asked.

"They have very little, Mark. From my understanding, they have more on you, Mark, than they have on Tony."

Mark and Tony looked at each other in surprise.

"What can they possibly have on me?"

"They have you giving Slim some dope and him giving you some money."

Tony looked at Mark. "I ain't give him a damn thing!" Then Mark thought back to when he and Joyce were down on Butler Street. Slim gave Mark a hundred dollars to give to Tommy. Mark leaned over toward Tony and in a low tone told Tony, "A few days ago I was down on Butler Street and Slim gave me a hundred dollars to give to Tommy."

Mr. Goodman interrupted. "What was that that you just told Tony?"

Mark answered. "I was telling Tony that a few days ago Slim gave me a hundred dollars to give to a friend of ours and introduced me to his friend, Joe."

"That must be Joseph Sheldon. Narcotics detective," Mr. Goodman said.

"That mother fucker's trying to set me up!" I screamed out.

Mr. Goodman said, "A year ago, you and Tony walked into my office and gave me $50,000. I remember asking what kind of case do you have. Mark, your reply was, 'None. This money is for if we ever do get a case.' I'm going to stay on top of this and keep my ears open and be ready to fight these sons of bitches, if and when they come up with a case. Now you and Tony don't worry too much because they don't have enough to make a case right now. And I can't see them exposing their hand to let you know that you are under investigation. And if I didn't have an insider in the prosecution office, we wouldn't know this much."

"Well, Mr. Goodman, we sure appreciate you calling us down here and giving us a run down on what's happening. Tony and I both were confused and puzzled as to what you had wanted to talk to us about. We were in the process of relocating to Atlanta to open up a company there. We had intended to get in touch with you to have your firm liquidate some properties."

Mr. Goodman said, "We have attorneys that deal strictly in businesses. You and Tony make out a list of the properties that you want liquidated and their locations and I'll get one of our attorneys on it right away."

"Okay, we'll send our girls down with the list in the next couple of days."

"Fine, Mark, that'll work. And if I were you, I wouldn't worry too much about the investigation at this time. They don't have anything solid enough to get an indictment yet."

"Thanks, Mr. Goodman. You have our numbers if anything comes up. When our girls come down with the list, they'll have the numbers for us in Atlanta."

Tony and I got up and walked out of the office.

In the car, Tony asked, "Well, Mark, what do you think?"

I leaned back with both hands on the steering wheel. "As of now, we're cool, but as far as what's going to happen later, it's up in the air," I said.

"Maybe we need to get somebody to take care of Slim," Tony suggested.

"I think you are right. He's the one that's trying to bring us down. Then the asshole tried to set me up by introducing me to the goddamn police as his friend. And I shook both of their damn hands. Yeah, Tony, he's got to go down!"

"Do you want me to put someone on him, Mark?"

"No, I'm gonna put Jerome and the new guy Richard on it."

"Are you sure that you want to put Richard on it? We've never used him for anything like that before."

"That's Jerome's friend and Jerome said that he's a beast and that he is down for anything. And if Jerome is comfortable with him, then maybe we should let them work together."

"Well, Mark, we know what Jerome is about. But we really don't know that much about Richard. If you think that's the best move, then go with it."

"Listen, Tony, I'm going to stop by Jerome's house now and talk about this."

Twenty minutes later...

We pulled up in front of Jerome's house. I parked and blew my horn several times. Jerome's wife opened the door.

"Jerome is not here, he's on Butler Street," she said.

We quickly pulled off.

As we rode down to Butler Street, I saw Jerome in front of the poolroom. I yelled out his name. He looked over and saw Tony and me sitting in the car. He walked over to us. "Jerome, you got a moment?"

"Sure, Tony."

"Have a seat in the car. We just left your house. Your wife told us that you were down here. We were headed to the bar-b-que joint when Mark spotted you over here."

"Yeah, baby, Shotgun was supposed to have shown up so that I could win some more of his money. Maybe he got cold feet. I've been waiting for over an hour. We were supposed to meet at 2 o'clock. It's now past 3 o'clock. So what is it that you want to talk about, Tony?"

"Actually, it's me and Mark that need to talk to you."

I cleared my throat and said, "You know that asshole Slim?"

"Ah, shit, what has he done?"

"Never mind what he did. He's got to go!"

"Well, Mark, if you say that he's got to go, he's got to go!"

I continued. "I want you and your friend Richard to snatch him and get rid of him." I then reached into my pocket and took out seven thousand dollars and I asked Tony to give me five thousand. I gave the twelve thousand to Jerome. "The seven thousand is for you. Give the five thousand to Richard and let me know when the job is finished."

Jerome put the money in his pockets. "Consider the job done!" He then got out of the car and I pulled off.

"Looks like our problem will be solved soon," I said to Tony.

Tony laughed and said, "Yeah, Mark, it looks like it will be."

On the way to drop Tony off, he wanted me to stop by some chick's house that he had met a couple of weeks ago. I pulled into the long driveway. Tony got out and went to the front door. I could see him ringing the doorbell. The door opened a few moments later. I couldn't make out the lady that he was talking to, but I could tell by Tony's movements and laughter that it was someone that he liked.

Tony leaned into the door and kissed her. The door closed and he walked to the car and got in. Tony smiled and said, "Drop me off at home."

I said, "Tony, when am I going to meet the mystery woman?"

"Soon, Mark, soon," he smiled.

"You know that we don't keep any secrets from each other."

"You'll meet her, Mark."

I dropped Tony off and went on home to spend some time with my lovely Joyce. We had just finished watching a movie and the news came on. I love watching my news. There was this reporter, with police cars and flashing lights. Sirens were wailing. It was on the corner of Washington and 57th. He was reporting on a shootout. The police were attempting to rescue an informant by the name of Raymond Little in an apparent kidnapping. The reporter went on.

"Little, forty years old, who was in the front passenger seat, was shot and killed. It was unclear who shot him. Nine detectives and police swooped in after receiving a phone call from Mr. Little's wife, saying that he had been kidnapped."

Joyce started to say something. I quieted her by saying, "Sshhh."

According to the police, they surrounded the vehicle with five of their cars. "The driver, Mr. Jerome Edwards, rammed one of the police cars in an attempt to get away. He then tried to hit one of the police officers. The police officers fired eight to nine rounds into the vehicle, killing Mr. Edwards. As he crashed into a fence, Mr. Richard James emerged from the back seat with gun in hand, firing twice. Police returned fire, hitting James three times, once in the abdomen, once in the shoulder and once in the leg.

"Mr. James was in and out of consciousness when the ambulance took him away. We will update you on his condition as soon as we know more."

The telephone rang. I answered it. "Hello."

"Hello, Mark. Mark, this is Tony. Are you watching the news?"

"Yeah, man, I'm watching it. Jerome is dead."

"Yeah and that damn Slim too! We've got to look out for Jerome's wife and kids."

"Yeah, we are going to definitely look out for them, Tony."

"I guess that we'll have to wait and see if Richard is going to make it. On the news they said that he was going in and out of consciousness."

"Well, I'll talk to you later, Tony."

We both hung up. Things had been getting pretty heated around Lansing. Just recently they had made a two hundred seventy-two thousand dollar heroin drug bust. And now a hit on Slim that went wrong.

Jerome is dead and Richard is fighting for his life. I turned to Joyce and said, "Baby, you and Brenda will be going to Atlanta, but before you leave, you are going to have to drop this list of properties off to Mr. Goodman's office. Drop the papers off on Friday, because you both will be leaving on Saturday. When you get to Atlanta, run an ad for a live-in housekeeper. She will live in the maid's quarters. Be sure to pick someone that we can work with."

"Is there anything else that you need me to do, honey?"

"No, I can't think of anything else, baby."

The next day, I went and picked up Tony. I said, "Tony, I was thinking last night after getting off the phone with you. Neither you nor I have any experience dealing with diamonds. Now I was thinking about Davis Jewelry, the place where we buy our diamonds from. Every time that we've gone into his store, he complained about how his competitors were squeezing him out of business. I was thinking about having him run things for us since he knows how to set up a business. And he knows diamonds."

Tony nodded. "Let's go down and talk to him now."

"Cool, let's go."

We headed for Davis Jewelry store. We pulled into the shopping center and parked close to where the jewelry store was located. We went inside. Surprisingly, there were quite a few people in the store. Mr. Davis himself was waiting on a couple. Mr. Davis looked up and saw Tony and me and said, "I'll be with you in a minute."

"Take your time, Mr. Davis, we are not in a hurry," I said.

Once Mr. Davis finished with his customer, he came over. "Hello, Mark. Hello, Tony. What can I interest you in today?"

"Sir, it's not what you can interest us in. It's what we can interest you in. We have a business proposition for you, if we can have a few minutes of your time. Do you have some place where we can talk?" I asked.

"A business proposition. What kind of business proposition are you talking about?"

"You are having financial problems and we have lots of money."

"Come on back into my office and we can talk." He turned to his employees. "Jackie, will you and Glen be alright until I get back?"

"Sure, Mr. Davis, we can handle it," she answered.

Tony, Mr. Davis and I walked back to his office. Mr. Davis offered us a seat then asked, "Now what is this business deal that you are offering?"

"Well, Mr. Davis, Tony and I are relocating to Atlanta. We have a business associate that can get us an unlimited supply of diamonds. Straight out of Sierra Leone. The best quality stones. We want to wholesale diamonds plus we want to open a real nice jewelry store."

"Oh, my God. Wholesale diamonds. You must be getting them awfully cheap."

"Yes, sir. Our only problem is that neither Tony nor myself have any experience with diamonds."

"So what can I do for you?" Mr. Davis asked.

"We are offering you a chance to become very wealthy. We know that you are knowledgeable in the diamond business and that you know other precious stones."

"Didn't you say that your company was going to be in Atlanta?" Mr. Davis asked.

"That's right. We are asking you to relocate. We'll take care of everything."

"Listen, Tony and Mark. I'm not trying to be smart or anything, but it will be very difficult to get that big of a loan from a bank for what you are trying to do. What I'm saying is, I am a white man who's been in business for fifteen years and banks are more partial to whites than blacks and I can't get a loan of that size."

"We don't need the banks to give us a loan. We have the money ourselves!"

"Mark, I don't think that you and Tony understand. What you are talking about will take a lot of money."

Tony and I looked at each other and smiled. We then looked back at Mr. Davis and said, "We have a lot of money! So what do you say?"

"I'll do it, but I have to pay bills before I can go."

"How much do you owe?" Tony asked.

Mr. Davis scratched his head. "Oh, I don't know. About fifteen, sixteen thousand."

Tony reached inside of his suit coat pocket and pulled out a brown envelope and tossed it on the desk. "Inside of there is thirty thousand in hundred dollar bills to take care of your business."

Mr. Davis picked up the envelope and looked inside of it. "Jesus, you guys are serious!"

"Yes, sir, very serious," Tony said.

Mr. Davis then asked, "What about my employees, Jackie and Glen? I've taught them everything that they know."

"Talk to them and see if they will relocate too. We will triple their salary and give them managerial jobs and pay the first six months' rent for any apartment that they choose."

"Oh, my God! I've prayed for something like this to happen." Mr. Davis was overjoyed.

"We would like for you to accompany us to Atlanta in a couple of days. We will check into the Hyatt Regency on Peachtree Street. We will pay the rent up for two weeks. We will find the proper attorney to draw the papers up for us. It will appear that you are the owner of the company. Tony and I will be in the shadows of the company. We will make you a very wealthy man. Once in Atlanta, Tony and I will have to leave for about a week to pick up the diamonds. We want you to find a place that will become our company."

Mr. Davis asked, "What about my inventory?"

"Pack up everything and store it. We will buy out your complete inventory and ship it to Atlanta. Any questions, Mr. Davis?"

"No. I'll talk to Jackie and Glen. I'll tell them what you told me."

We got up and shook hands. Everyone said, "Partners," and we left the store.

I dropped Tony off at home and I went on home. I wanted to spend some time with Joyce before she had to go to Atlanta. The evening went well. Brenda called and asked Joyce if she was packed and ready to go? Joyce said that she was all packed and anxious to get back to Atlanta and start her new life. They were still talking when I dozed off to sleep.

Friday came quickly. That morning, Joyce was going to pick Brenda up and drop off the list to the lawyer's office. The next day they would be leaving for Atlanta. Tony, Mr. Davis and I would be leaving today for Atlanta. I called Tony and asked if he was ready to go pick up Mr. Davis.

"I should be at your house in about fifteen minutes, Tony, and we can pick up Mr. Davis and head for the airport."

I picked up Tony and Mr. Davis. I drove to the airport where we all boarded the plane, headed for Atlanta.

Chapter Eleven

One week later...

Joyce had interviewed several housekeepers since she'd been in Atlanta. She'd hired a middle-aged woman, a really sweet woman. Joyce was really happy. I could see the gleam in her eyes.

When I talked to Tony, he would say the same about Brenda. Tony and I had gone by the Hyatt Regency Hotel several times and Mr. Davis seemed to be really enjoying himself.

Mr. Davis enjoyed the fitness center and the sauna. In the evening he would have a gourmet dinner in the restaurant. Then he would have drinks in the bar, where they had a gorgeous blonde blues singer who was accompanied by an older, tuxedo wearing gentleman playing a huge, white baby grand piano.

I'd called Joy a few times since I'd been in Atlanta. She really missed me and I was missing her as well. I asked Tony if he'd talked to his mystery woman, the one that he hadn't introduced me to yet. I also asked if he was going to bring her to Atlanta? He looked at me and smiled without saying a word. But I knew it meant that she would be coming. I know my partner so well, and he knows me. That's probably why we do so well together.

A couple of days later, Tony and I picked up Mr. Davis. We met with attorney Terry Jones at his office. He was recommended to me by my attorney, Mr. Goodman, from Lansing. When we walked into his office, I introduced myself. I said, "Mr. Jones, my name is Mark Jones and this is my partner, Tony Moore, and our associate, Mr. Davis."

"Mark, I see that we have something in common, our last names are the same."

"Yes, sir. I hope that means that we can work well together," I said.

"I don't see why not. Mr. Goodman has already run down to me what you guys need. Now this is what I'm going to do. First off, do you have a name for this corporation?"

"We were going to name it Diamonds Unlimited, Inc., but instead, we are going to name it M&J Rare Jewelers, Inc."

I looked over at Tony. He smiled and said, "Good name."

Mr. Terry Jones said, "I am going to set this company up where it shows Mr. Davis to be the owner. But actually, Mark, you and Tony are the real owners. Mr. Davis will appear to be the owner, just on the surface. I will make myself an officer of the corporation. Whereas all paper trail will stop on my desk. I should have you all incorporated within a few days." Mr. Terry Jones paused for a moment. Then he asked, "Have you found a location since you've been here?"

Tony answered, "No, sir, we are letting Mr. Davis find a location for us. Mark and I will be leaving town soon on some other business. We were hoping that you know someone to assist Mr. Davis in finding the property that we need."

Mr. Terry Jones paused again. He raised his finger to his temple as if he was thinking. He then said, "I have the right person for you. One of my law secretaries used to be a real estate agent. And I'm sure that she still has connections. Hold on a moment while I call her in." He picked up the phone and spoke into it. "Doris, can you please tell Diane to step back here for a moment."

Diane came into the office. "Yes, sir, did you want to see me?"

"Yes, Diane. I have these clients that are trying to find a building that can house a large jewelry store and a wholesale precious stone business over top of it or beside it. They will pay you for your services. Do you think that you will be able to show Mr. Davis around?"

"Sure, Mr. Jones. Where are you staying, Mr. Davis?" Diane asked.

"I am staying at the Hyatt Regency on Peachtree. Do you know where that's at?" Mr. Davis asked.

"Yes, I know where that is. Will you be ready tomorrow?" Diane asked.

"Yes, tomorrow will be fine. What time can you pick me up, Diane?"

"I'll come and get you at nine in the morning. We'll get an early start."

"Fine!" Mr. Davis said. "I'll be ready."

Diane then said, "It's been nice meeting you gentlemen. Mr. Davis, I'll see you in the morning," then she left the office.

Diane was a beautiful woman that looked to be Italian. She had long, dark hair with dark brown eyes. She had an olive complexion and was very shapely. She had a sweet personality.

"Mr. Jones, we'd like for you to be our attorney on payroll all year long. You give us a reasonable fee and Mr. Davis will pay you tomorrow," Tony said.

We all stood up to leave and shook hands and said, "It's a pleasure doing business."

We left the office and dropped Mr. Davis off at his hotel. We told him that if he needed any more money to contact Joyce or Brenda. We handed him our numbers and left.

On the way to drop Tony off, I said to him, "Looks like it's all coming together now."

Tony said, "Have faith, Mark."

I said to Tony, "I know, baby. It's gonna be alright."

The next day...

Before leaving for New York, I decided to call Eugene and asked how Richard was doing. He said that they had recovered two of the bullets and that one had gone through his arm. He's out of the hospital, but he's in county jail being held without bail on first-degree murder charges. I asked Eugene if he had hired a good attorney for Richard. Eugene said, "Yes, I've hired two attorneys."

"Good, what are they saying?" I asked.

"They are saying that this is going to be a tough case. He was shot getting out of the car with his gun in hand firing at the police. And this Raymond Little guy was shot from behind, while sitting in the front seat. The problem is that Richard was sitting in the back seat and Jerome was driving the car. Mark, it don't look good."

"Did you take Richard some money, Eugene?" Mark asked.

"Yes, I did all of that."

"If there is anything that he needs, make sure that he gets it," I said. "Tell him that I said to stay strong and that we are going to try and beat this thing. If not, that we can at least get it down to something he can live with. Tell him that we are going to be there for him, always! How's everything else going? How's Tommy, Dollar Bill, Curtis and Earl doing?"

"Everybody is cool, taking care of their business."

"What about Margo?" Mark asked.

"Margo is good. She misses you and Tony," Eugene said.

"Tell Margo that we love her and that we will be calling her soon."

"Sure will, Mark," and they both said good bye and hung up.

I called Tony and asked him if he was ready to go. We had two hours before our flight was scheduled to leave. I then went and picked up Tony. On the way to the airport, I said, "Tony, I called Eugene. Richard is out of the hospital. He's in the county jail being held without bail."

"Mark, did Eugene get Richard an attorney?"

"Yes, he got him two good attorneys and he left him plenty of money on the books. Tony, this looks like a tight case for the prosecution. This might be a hard one to beat."

"I hope that Richard can stand up to all of the pressure, Mark."

"I hope so too, Tony, this was Jerome's man."

"I guess that this is a wait and see thing, Mark."

"Yeah, I know."

We had just parked. We got out and removed our luggage. We hopped on a shuttle cart and rode it into the terminal. The terminal was huge. People were everywhere, hurrying from place to place trying to catch their flights. We flew first class on Delta Airlines. A non-stop flight into J.F.K. Airport inside New York City. We took a cab to the Algonquin Hotel and Fifth Avenue. We had reservations for two suites.

The Nigerians were at the Marriott Hotel on Broadway. After getting settled in, we called Solako and Kamara and agreed to meet them at their hotel. We agreed to meet them at 9 p.m. Tony and I had wanted to go check out the luxury spa and get a massage. We both liked facials too. I called both of my women up. Joyce said that she was just doing little things around the house all day. She really liked Atlanta and repeated a question that she'd been asking all week. How long were we going to be gone? I answered her saying, "As long as it takes."

And then I said to her, "Baby, I'm going to have to go. I've got a business engagement in about an hour. I love you, Joyce."

"I love you back." She gave me a kiss through the telephone and we hung up.

I called Joy as well. She was telling me how much she missed me. I asked her if she was alright. If she needed anything.

She said, "No baby, I'm fine. I still have plenty of money left from the money that you gave me."

"How are your mother are father? And your little brother and sister?" I asked.

"They are all doing fine," she said.

"Tell all of them that I said hello."

"I will, baby."

"I love you, Joy. I'll call you back in a couple of days."

"I love you too, Mark." We both hung up.

Tony was in his suite, touching base at home as well. He and Brenda were very much in love just as Joyce and I were. Brenda and Joyce had become very close. They loved to shop together. And they loved for the four of us to go out and party from time to time.

"Listen, Brenda, if Mr. Davis calls and needs anything, give it to him. But keep track of what he gets. Mark and I gave him both yours and Joyce's phone numbers. He is trying to locate the right property for our business. We have hired a young lady that works for our attorney in Atlanta. She's a law clerk for him. She used to be a real estate agent, so we should come up with something really soon. Now you and Joyce know our tastes, so I want the both of you to look at it too. And if it's cool, then do whatever needs to be done. I love you, baby."

"I love you too."

"Mark is probably waiting on me so I have to go. Bye, love."

"Bye," and they both hung up.

Tony left his suite and knocked on my door. I opened the door. He was dressed and ready to go.

"I see that you are ready," Tony said.

"Yeah, man, I've got everything." I held up the briefcase.

We went down the elevator and the doorman hailed a cab for us. We headed to the Marriott Hotel to meet with Solako and Kamara. We arrived at their hotel and took the elevator up to Solako's room. We knocked on the door. Moments later, a huge African looking man let us both inside the room.

"Tony, it is so very good to see you, my friend." Mr. Solako greeted Tony with a wide grin and a hug. He then turned toward me. "And you must be Mark. It's good to finally meet you, Mark. Tony speaks so very highly of you. Have a seat, my friends. Would you care for some refreshments?"

"No, thank you, Mr. Solako," Tony said.

"Well, let me call Kamara and have him bring the stones to the room. You must have something in the briefcase for us?"

"Yes, we do," Tony said. "Two hundred fifty thousand dollars in U.S. currency."

Solako then picked up the phone and spoke into the receiver. "They are here. You can bring that over to my room now."

Five minutes later, there was a knock on the door. Mr. Solako answered the door and Kamara came in.

"Tony, Tony, my friend. So very good to see you once again. So I see that I get the pleasure of meeting Mark."

"Stand up, Mark," Kamara said. Kamara pulled me close in the traditional greeting. He went cheek to cheek with me, then we all sat at the table next to the bed. Kamara lay a black velvet cloth across the table. He pulled a black velvet case out of his inside pocket. He opened it and laid the beautiful white diamonds on the black velvet cloth.

Tony and I were examining the diamonds. We had never seen so many beautiful, loose diamonds before.

I sat the briefcase on the table and opened it. Then slid it over to Solako and Kamara and said, "Would you like to count it?"

Solako closed the briefcase and said, "No need, Mark, we are friends."

"Very well, Mr. Solako, it was a pleasure doing business with you. We will see you again soon."

Everybody got up and walked to the door.

Solako leaned over and whispered into Tony's ear, "I like your friend, Mark. Maybe we can come to Atlanta the next time that we do business. Have you set your company up yet?"

"Everything should be in place by the next time that we do business," Tony said.

"Very well, Tony," Solako said. "And it was a pleasure meeting you, Mark!"

Kamara added, "Indeed, indeed it was!"

Both of us walked out the door. We caught a cab and went back to the Algonquin Hotel. We got back to the hotel and stopped at the desk and asked to rent a safe deposit box.

We were sitting up in Tony's suite talking. I suggested to Tony, "Maybe we should turn this into a little vacation since we are done with our business. It will be a well-deserved vacation. We have been really working hard these past couple of years. I can send for Joy and maybe I can finally get to meet your mystery girl. So what do you think, Tony?"

Tony thought for a minute, then he smiled and said, "Why not. Let's stay for a while. Brenda and Joyce are handling things in Atlanta. Plus this will give us an opportunity to see how they handle things without us there."

"You're right, Tony, they haven't really been tested up under pressure. In order for us to succeed, we have to have strong women behind us. That's a good idea. A very good idea."

"I agree with you, Mark," Tony said. Tony picked up the phone and dialed his mystery woman. "Hello, Renee." He looked at me and smiled. "Renee, this is Tony."

"Hi, Tony, baby. Are you in Atlanta?"

"No, sweetheart, I'm in New York."

"But I thought that you were moving to Atlanta?" Renee said.

"I did, sweetheart. I'm in New York taking care of some business. My friend, Mark and I. But now we are done on the business end and we were talking about bringing our girls up here for a couple of weeks. Would you like to come up and spend some time with me?"

"Oh, Tony, can I? I would love to come to New York and spend some time with you. I've never been to New York before. They say that it's the city that never sleeps. Oh, Tony, when can I come?" she begged.

"What about tomorrow? Maybe you could fly up with Mark's girl. I'm going to give you her phone number before we hang up, but don't call her for at least an hour. Mark hasn't called her yet to see if she's coming."

"Baby, what do I need to bring?" Renee asked.

"You don't have to bring anything, sweetheart. You can go and shop for whatever you want when you get here. Just bring your beautiful self."

"Oh, Tony, you are so sweet. You always know what to say to make a girl feel good."

"Write down this phone number, baby. 481-2280. Mark's woman's name is Joy. She'll be waiting for your call. Alright, baby, I have to go now. I love you."

"I love you too, Tony," Renee said, hanging up the phone.

By this time I was in my suite talking to Joy. "So, baby, you and Tony's woman are going to catch a flight out tomorrow. She'll be calling you shortly. Her name is Renee. There is no need to pack a lot of clothes, Joy, you can do all of the shopping that you'll like once you get here."

"Mark, I can't wait to see you. I miss you so much."

"I miss you too, baby. Which is why I'm bringing you here to New York to spend some time with me before you move to Atlanta."

"Move to Atlanta! Oh, baby, you didn't tell me that you were going to move me to Atlanta!"

"You didn't think that I would leave you in Lansing while I'm living in Atlanta? Joy, I love you. You are my woman and I want you near me at all times."

"Oh, Mark, that's so sweet and I want to be there for you whenever you need me."

"Okay, sweetheart, when you get to the airport have a cab bring you to the Algonquin Hotel. Stop at the desk and ask for our rooms. Mark Jones and Tony Moore. The desk will be expecting you. Take the elevator to the nineteenth floor. I am in suite 1948 and Tony is in suite 1950. We should be there when you get there. But if we're not in, just hang around. We'll be in shortly. Okay, you got all of that, baby?"

"Yes, sweetheart, I've got it."

"Okay, Joy, I love you and I'll see you once you get here."

"I love you too, Mark. Bye," Joy said, hanging up the phone.

I immediately dialed Tony's room and told him that I had just gotten off the phone with Joy. Tony said that he'd talked to Renee and that she was going to call Joy. I said, "Cool, I'll talk to you, baby," and we both hung up.

Chapter Twelve

The next evening...

Tony and I were at the fitness center. After working out, we both went up to my suite. As we stepped in, we heard female voices. We walked deeper into the suite and saw Joy and Renee. They got up and immediately ran over to our arms. We all embraced and kissed. I stepped back and looked at my woman and said, "I missed you, beautiful!" then I turned toward Tony and Renee.

"So I finally get to meet the mystery woman." Both Tony and Renee smiled.

Renee was gorgeous. She had large, hazel, oval shaped eyes. Her skin was smooth. She had a light complexion and a very shapely body. She reminded me of Lena Horn, the entertainer. Absolutely gorgeous!

That evening we sat around in my suite and kicked it for a while. Later that night, Tony and Renee went to their suite.

The next morning we had breakfast in our suite. Tony and Renee joined us for breakfast. We ate and kidded around We all laughed and had a good time. We were both happy that we'd sent for our women.

The suite was now filled with a positive energy. Everyone seemed so alive and happy. The excitement that the girls had felt brought joy to me and to Tony as well. We saw how happy they were and it made us feel good.

"So, are you girls ready to go see the Big Apple and do some shopping?" Tony asked.

Joy looked at me with a big smile on her face. I just smiled back, then Joy said, "Yes, yes we are! Aren't we, Renee?"

Renee looked at Tony then at Joy and said, "We certainly are!"

"Well, Mark, are you ready?" Tony asked me.

I slowly got up and said, "I guess so."

Everybody laughed as we walked out of the suite and got on the elevator. We listened to the sounds of Louis Armstrong as we rode the elevator down to the lobby. We asked the red-uniformed bellhop to hail a cab for us.

Once the cab arrived, we all went out to get in. Tony slipped the bellhop a little tip as he walked past him.

The first stop was Saks Fifth Avenue. They bought several outfits from Saks, then continued on shopping across the garment district. Soon it was time for lunch. We went to Sylvia's Restaurant up in Harlem where they have very good food. Some of everyone has eaten there at one time or other. Movie stars and entertainers stop by sometime whenever they are in town and it's not uncommon to see politicians there also.

We were seated and enjoyed a great lunch. Joy and I had smothered pork chops, macaroni and cheese, collared greens and corn bread. For dessert, we both had peach cobbler.

Tony had Salisbury steak with mashed potatoes and green beans. Renee wanted fried chicken with mashed potatoes and macaroni and cheese. For dessert, Tony and Renee both had heated Dutch apple pie with a scoop of vanilla ice cream. We all drank iced tea with our meals.

When we left, we were so full that we could hardly move. We decided to go back to the hotel and chill out for a while.

Lansing, Michigan...

Seated in the interrogation room at the police station were Detective Joe Whitfield and Sergeant Ted Frederick of the homicide division, waiting on the deputies to bring murder suspect Richard James in for questioning.

While waiting, Prosecutor Roland Hindenburg walked in. "Did you send for the suspect yet?" the prosecutor asked.

"Yes," answered Sergeant Frederick. "They are bringing him down now."

"Get this bastard to implicate Mark Jones! And Tony Moore too, if possible," Prosecutor Hindenburg said.

A few moments later...

Richard James entered the room handcuffed, shackled and escorted by two large white deputies.

"Have a seat, Mr. James," Detective Whitfield said.

Prosecutor Hindenburg opened his briefcase and took a tape recorder out of it. He set it up on the table and sat several blank tapes next to it. He picked up one tape and inserted it into the tape recorder and pushed record.

"Mr. James, you know why we are here. And this is a chance for you to save your own ass! You are facing life and I'm sure you'll get it, once you're convicted of the murder of Raymond Little! Now, your friend, Jerome Edwards, is dead. And we know that Jerome worked for Mark Jones and Tony Moore. We also know that they are responsible for the majority of the heroin in our city. So if you'll help us put those two away, we will probably be able to get you a five to fifteen year sentence with you getting out in three. That would be a manslaughter charge, am I right, Mr. Hindenburg?"

"That is correct, Mr. Frederick."

"So what do you say, Mr. James? Are you ready to work with us?" the prosecutor asked, sitting back, crossing his arms.

"What is it that you want me to do?" Richard asked.

Mr. Frederick paced back and forth in front of Richard as he sat calmly in the seat. "We want you to say that it was Mark Jones and Tony Moore that gave you and Jerome Edwards the contract to kill informant Raymond Little!"

"Well, sir, I can't do that! Nobody gave us a contract to kill this man. It was a dispute over some money that he and Jerome had. I can't tell you if Jerome shot him or not. But I know that I didn't."

"Listen, mother fucker!!! I'm tired of fooling around with you, you piece of shit! If you don't say that Mark Jones and Tony Moore gave you the contract to kill Raymond Little, your black ass is going down! And you will never see daylight again! Either way, your two nigger friends are going down!!"

"Sergeant Frederick, what you are asking me to do is lie!" Richard said.

"You're damn right, you son of a bitch! Is that recorder running?"

Detective Whitfield looked over at the recorder and said, "Yes, it's running, prosecutor."

"Then turn that damn thing off! And put a new tape in."

The detective removed the unmarked tape and threw it into the prosecutor's briefcase.

"What are you going to do, Mr. Richards?"

"I'm sorry, but I can't do that. I can't implicate these men on something that they had nothing to do with. Plus, I think that the bullet that killed Raymond came from one of your guns anyhow."

"Get this fucker out of my sight. I'm tired of looking at him!"

The detectives called for the deputies to take Mr. James back to his cell.

New York City...

The girls had been with us for a week now. We've done so many things this week. We enjoyed a carriage ride through Central Park. The sun was shining. There were lots of people moving about. Later we went to see The King and I starring Yul Bruner. It was a great show. Afterwards we went back to the hotel. We decided to hang around the hotel lounge and have a few drinks. There was an excellent four-piece jazz band. We sat down and swayed to the music. Everyone was enjoying themselves.

A few moments later, the waitress came to our table. She was a short-stacked redhead with freckles all over her face. She asked, "What would you like to drink?"

I immediately said, "You can bring me a cherry coke with plenty of cherries in it." I then asked Joy, "What would you like?" Joy ordered a strawberry daiquiri. I then asked Renee what she would like? Renee ordered Tanquary and lime. And Tony ordered Hennessey.

Tony said, "Mark, jazz is really soothing, isn't it?"

"Yes, I like it. It relaxes me. I also like it when I'm on the road traveling. You know, Joy has a whole collection of jazz albums."

"Girl, is that true?" Renee asked.

Joy looked at me and smiled. Then she said, "Yes, I have a pretty big collection."

"Tony, before we leave New York, maybe we will hit a blues club. Do y'all like blues?"

Tony said, "I really like going to blues clubs. The women get to drinking and singing along and the next thing you know, they are crying over their men." Tony and I started laughing.

"And some of the men get drunk and start crying over their women too!" Renee said while kissing Tony on the cheek. She smiled and winked at Joy.

We ordered a couple rounds of drinks. We were really having a pleasant time. It was really nice having the girls with us. The evening was winding down. After being on the go all day, we decided to go back to our suites.

I paid for the drinks and tipped the waitress. Then we took the elevator back up to my suite. Tony and Renee stopped in for a moment.

We were all sitting down on the couch and the chair. I excused myself to make a phone call. I said that I needed to call my sister. Everyone looked surprised. I heard Tony mumble as I walked away, "His sister?"

I picked up the phone and dialed the number. The phone rang three times. Then someone answered. "Hello."

"Hi, Sis, this is Mark."

Her voice was filled with excitement as she said, "Hello, Mark, how are you doing? I'm glad that you called. How is Atlanta?"

"Atlanta is good. But I'm not in Atlanta right now. I'm in New York City. My friend and I are here on business."

"Are you talking about Tony? The friend that you have been telling me about when you call?"

"Yes, Sis, that's him. Listen, tomorrow I'm going to send you some more money."

"I still have some money left from the last time that you sent me some."

"It doesn't matter. I want you to always have whatever you need, Sis. Well, Sis, I have to go now. I'm sorry for waking you up this early in the morning."

"Don't be sorry. I always want to hear from you, no matter what time it is."

"Alright, Sis, I've got to go now. Bye."

"Bye, Mark," she said, hanging up the phone.

I walked back to where everyone was sitting. Tony was looking at me puzzled. "Mark, you never told me that you had a sister," Tony said.

"I'm sorry, Tony. I thought that I had mentioned it to you before. But maybe I didn't. I have always tried to keep my sister on the low because of my lifestyle. One day we will go to Ohio together and you will get a chance to meet her, Tony. You, too, Joy." I yawned. "I know that everybody is tired. At least I am. What do you all want to do tomorrow?"

"We know what the girls want to do. They want to shop," Tony said.

"I'm talking about later on that evening?" Mark said.

"We are here in New York City. Why not go to the Apollo?" Joy said.

"Sounds good, Joy. Sounds good to me. Then tomorrow, the Apollo it is."

The next day, the girls wanted to do a little shopping. We all ate breakfast together, then we went our separate ways. Tony and I went to the fitness center while they girls went shopping. We went swimming then we went back up to our rooms. We sat around and kicked it for a minute. Then Tony decided to go downstairs and see if the bellhop knew where we could get four tickets to the famous Apollo Theater.

The bellhop said yes, he knew where to get the tickets. So Tony gave him the money for the tickets and came back up to my room.

A couple of hours later, the bellhop came and knocked on the door. I answered the door. The bellhop came in holding the four tickets in his hand. "Here are the tickets to the Apollo that your friend asked me to get."

"Thanks, my man," I said as he handed the tickets to me.

"Great," said Tony, who was sitting in the chair.

I hit the bellhop off with a fifty dollar bill. "Thank you, sir, is there anything else that I can do for you? If so, just let me know."

"No, thank you, but that's all for now," I said. Then I let him out.

It wasn't a half an hour later that the girls returned carrying armloads of bags from Bloomingdale's and Saks Fifth Avenue. Clothes from all of the top designers filled the bags. I suggested that everyone go and get some rest for the big night tonight. I asked if anybody wanted to go downstairs and eat or just call room service. We decided to eat dinner in my suite after we got a couple of hours sleep.

Three hours later, everyone was rested and dressed. Tony and Renee came back over to my suite. We all ate big meals, but we didn't stuff ourselves. We didn't want to seem sluggish and tired before we went out.

I decided that it would be a good idea to call Eugene to see how our business was doing back in Lansing before we left. I said, "Tony, I'm going to call Eugene to see how he is doing back in Lansing."

"Good idea," said Tony.

"I also want to find out how Richard is holding up."

I picked up the phone and dialed Eugene's number. The phone rang several times before he answered. "Hello."

"Eugene, this is Mark."

"Mark, baby! How are you doing? How is Atlanta?"

"I'm doing good, Eugene. Atlanta is sweet. I love it here."

Eugene asked, "Is Tony there with you?"

"Yes, he's here."

"Tell him that I said hey."

"Tony, Eugene said to tell you hey."

"Tell Eugene that I'll be there in about a month to pick that up," Tony said.

"Eugene, Tony will be there next month to pick that up."

"Alright, Mark, it will all be right as usual."

"Okay, baby, that was one of the reasons that I called. I also wanted to know how Richard is holding up?"

"He's cool, Mark. His woman goes to see him regularly. He sends messages by her to me."

"What about the lawyers?" I asked.

"Well, they are doing the best that they can with what they have. You know that Slim was shot from behind and Richard was the only one sitting in the back seat. To add to that, he jumped out of the back seat and fired two rounds at the police before they could take him down. The lawyer is hoping that the prosecutor will make a deal instead of going to trial. But those arrogant bastards are walking around with their confidence level at an all-time high. The lawyers believe that the prosecutor has something else in mind. You and Tony. Richard said that the detectives and the prosecutor came at him once already, but he told them that he didn't know anything."

"So, Eugene, what you are saying is that they tried to squeeze him?"

"No, what I'm saying is that they have a vice grip on his ass."

"Well, that shouldn't be a problem because we never talked to him about anything. We only talked to Jerome and Jerome is dead. Dead men tell no tales."

"I heard that, baby."

"Okay, Eugene, I'm going to have to hang up now. We'll be in touch with you."

"Alright, see you, Mark." And we both hung up.

I pulled Tony into the other room and gave him the rundown on what Eugene had just told me. When we talked to

Jerome, Richard wasn't even around, so there is nothing that he can say about us.

"We should be cool then, Mark," Tony said, "as long as they don't get to this guy. We have to make sure that he has everything that he needs while he's in there."

"Well, Tony, we got him two damn good attorneys. I don't know what else that we can do for him." I paused for a moment. "Unless we get someone to do him."

"Well, we'll keep that option open. In the meantime, let's see how this plays out," Tony said.

"There is nothing that we can do at this point. Let's get the girls and go."

We walked into the room and I asked them, "Are you ready to go to the Apollo?"

Both girls jumped up and said, "Oh, yes, we are definitely ready to go!"

We left the suite and took the elevator down to the lobby where the bellhop called a cab for us.

It was amateur night at the Apollo. There was a lot of good talent there. We applauded the good talent and we booed the bad. The place was packed. It was a good thing that we had gotten our tickets early.

The girls really enjoyed themselves. It was their first time in New York City and the first time at the Apollo for all of us together. It was an enjoyable two weeks. But tomorrow we will all have to depart. Going separate ways. The girls will be going back to Lansing. Tony and I will be going back to Atlanta.

We left the Apollo and grabbed a late night snack at Sylvia's Restaurant. We then caught a cab and went back to our suites.

Tony and Renee were as tired as we were. They said goodnight and we went to our separate suites. Joy and I undressed for bed. The sight of her beautiful naked body made me forget how tired I was. We made mad passionate love, then fell asleep wrapped in each other's arms.

Chapter Thirteen

It was a good year for Tony and me. It was August 1977. Our jewelry store was doing great and our diamond wholesale business was also doing well. Richard had vigorously fought his case for two-and-a-half years. He did not prevail. We were able to get it dropped from first-degree murder to second-degree murder. He was no longer facing natural life. He was sentenced to fifteen to life. He will be eligible for parole in thirteen years. The lawyers immediately appealed the conviction. It is now a wait-and-see situation. Appeals can last anywhere from six months to years.

Richard has shown that he is a soldier. He has stood up throughout the entire ordeal. Our real obligation to Richard ended when Jerome accepted the money to fulfill the contract. But Tony and I always felt that we would never let a soldier drown that is fighting so hard to stay above water. Especially one that didn't grab us by the ankles and try to bring us under. We will definitely continue to support him and his family. We will also continue to look for angels to try and bring him home.

Joyce and Brenda had proven their worth. We let them oversee both businesses. Even though David is the one that truly knows diamonds, Joyce and Brenda had learned a lot from him. We do a lot of one-of-a-kind pieces. He is one impeccable craftsman. We have hustlers, pimps, singers and movie stars coming to buy pieces from us.

Joyce and Brenda are the managers of the companies. David is out front appearing as the owner, but all major decisions are made by Tony or me.

Tony and I often visit Auburn Avenue. That is the street where people of all walks of life come together. Street people. People like Tony and me. On every corner there is a liquor store. People filled the streets. Pimps and their ho's. Boosters, winos and people out just to see who else was out. Drug dealers were out selling bundles of heroin. A bundle went for sixty-five dollars. There were fifteen little cellophane packs. Each pack had a McDonalds spoonful of heroin in it.

There were bars and greasy spoon restaurants up and down the street. There was a poolroom that Tony and I liked to go to. It was next to a bar. Upstairs over the bar was a trick house where girls would turn their tricks.

Every so often you would see black plainclothes narcotics officers coming down the street, looking just like anyone else. They came in twos. These men were sometimes very brutal. They would take suspected dealers and make them strip butt naked in the doorways, searching them for drugs. And if they didn't respond quick enough, they would beat them down like animals.

I remember one hot muggy night, Tony and I had just pulled up. There were plainclothes police that were beating this man unmercifully. The man squealed like a pig that was getting slaughtered. Blood was everywhere. They applied so much force when they struck him with their clubs that a long split ran down his forehead.

This woman ran out screaming hysterically. I'm not sure if it was his wife or his woman. She begged the men to stop. "Please, stop," she shouted. "Somebody call the police."

They shoved her aside and said, "Bitch, we are the police. If you don't want some of this, then you had better get your nappy headed ass out of here."

I looked at Tony. He was shaking his head in disgust. I said to him, "Baby, how can we come up when our own people are beating us down? And they are inflicting on their own people the same injustice the white man has inflicted on all of us for the past four hundred years. See what happens when you give a black man a badge? He does us so bad that you won't even recognize him as a brother. Why is that, Tony?"

"It's because the black cop wants to be accepted so bad by the white cop that he'll beat his brother down so bad hoping that the white cop will embrace him. But all the time, the white cop looks at him as a sellout and a traitor to his own people. But he never let's on."

"You know, Tony, I'm so glad that we are like we are. Two young brothers with millions of dollars, who enjoy being around their own people. Not like the sellout niggers that get a little money and moves to an all-white suburb. Which is cool, but betraying their own people is wrong."

I remember another particular hot, muggy night while Tony and I were down on Auburn Avenue. We heard a loud ruckus upstairs over the bar. Suddenly, two people came tumbling down the stairs onto the sidewalk. The streets were packed. Everyone moved in to see if they could recognize who was fighting. Tony and I moved in too. It was a woman and a man. The woman had the man in a headlock. Her left arm was locked around his head, while she repeatedly punched the man in the face with her right hand.

Each punch landed squarely on the man's face. The man was hollering out loudly, but at first we couldn't make out what he was saying. Every time that he opened his mouth, her fist would find it. She pummeled this man's face until it was a bloody mess.

"Bitch! If you let me go, I'll beat your mother fuckin' ass," the man screamed in between the punches that she continually landed to his face. "Let me go, bitch, let me go!"

Then the woman did something that surprised us all. She let the bloodied man go. She stood up and put up her dukes. Ready to go at it again. "Okay, mother fucker, let's fight!" she said.

Then, without warning, the man turned and ran down the street. Before he took off, we recognized that it was Silky, a pimp friend of ours that we had met a year ago.

Silky was a short, unattractive pimp with a stable of fine white bitches. Tony often wondered how Silky could come up with so many fine women. So one day, Tony took it upon himself to ask the question. I, myself, already knew the answer, because at one time, I was pimpin'. I knew that you didn't have to be attractive to be a pimp. It is embedded in you. Just like a painter that paints a beautiful picture and everyone standing around is admiring how beautiful it is. So does a pimp paint a picture for his ho's.

Then Tony asked Silky, "How do you come up with so many fine bitches to work for you?"

Silky stood back and placed both hands on his hips and looked Tony straight in his eyes and said, "What is my name?"

"It's Silky," Tony replied.

"That's right. Silky is my name. Pimping is my game, and anything else, need not be explained."

Out of respect, Silky didn't use the last two words to this sentence, which were, "...to a lame." So at that point, Tony didn't question it. He let it alone.

Silky has been very helpful to Tony and me in various ways. For instance, there was a motel down the street from the bar where all of the pimps, boosters, drug dealers, hustlers and dope fiends hung out. Silky introduced us to two top notched women boosters. Tony and I would come in and buy all of their merchandise for a third. They would have men's suits, women's suits, men's and women's leather coats. Men's and women's fur coats. After a while, other boosters heard of us and they wanted to start bringing their merchandise to us too.

Silky was telling us about a friend of his named Gerald. He was a little down on his luck. Silky said that Gerald was a good guy and he wanted us to meet him.

I asked Silky, "Where are you going with this?" He said, "You guys have been buying a lot of pieces from boosters and Gerald knows a lot of people. And Gerald also has a large home with a full basement that he could sell the pieces for you from. He's not working now and he and his wife are struggling. Maybe you guys can let Gerald move all of the pieces for you? That way he can make a few dollars for you and for himself."

I looked at Tony and asked him, "What do you think about this idea, Tony?"

"Well, Mark, we've been letting our ladies take what they want and pick out what we want then give the rest to our family and friends backing Lansing. Maybe we can make a business out of it. You know that all of the other boosters want to deal with us. Why not let this Gerald handle it for us? Maybe we can make some money out it. Silky, when can we meet this Gerald?"

"We can go by his house now, if you don't have anything else to do."

"Let's go," and we all got into Tony's 1977 Cadillac.

Fifteen to twenty minutes later we pulled up in front of Gerald's house. Silky said, "That's his house across the street. The white one with the blue trim.

I asked, "Do you want to go up and talk to him first?"

"No, Mark. I told you that my man is cool. It's just he and his wife. He had a son, but in 1974, his son got hit by a car and died. My friend was devastated from the loss and went into a deep depression. I was worried about him. I didn't know if he would ever come back to his self again. It took some time, but he finally came around."

"Look at you, Silky. A pimp with a compassionate heart," I said.

"I'm cold only toward my ho's 'cause that's my living, Mark. Come on, let's go in so you all can meet Gerald."

We all got out of the car. Tony locked the doors. We crossed the street and walked up onto the porch. Silky rang the doorbell. I heard the lock click and the door swung open. Gerald was standing there. "Silky, my man, come on in."

"Gerald, I want you to meet a couple of friends of mine. Gerald, this is Tony and Mark."

Tony shook Gerald's hand and said, "It's a pleasure meeting you." I shook his hand as well.

"Gerald, I brought these two gentlemen by to meet you. They have a business proposition that you may or may not be interested in."

"Why don't you all have a seat and let me hear this proposition."

"I introduced Tony and Mark to Linda and Carol, the two booster chicks at the motel on Auburn Avenue," Silky said.

"You mean the ones that was getting all of them nice pieces?"

"Yeah, that's them. Well, Tony and Mark had been buying all of their merchandise. Every booster in town wants to meet Tony and Mark, now. But they weren't interested because the girls were getting enough merchandise for them. That's when I brought you up. I know that you have been out of work for quite a while now, and you and your lovely wife are trying to keep up with your bills. I told them that you know everybody that is somebody in this town and that you could sell everything that they can come up with."

"Hell, I can sell a whole department store if they could get it."

"So does that mean that you are in?"

"You're damn right! I can use the money. Excuse me, let me call my wife in here. Honey, honey, can you come in here for a minute?"

A tall, dark complexioned, slender woman with a short Afro stepped into the room. She wasn't a beautiful woman, but she wasn't ugly either. She was just plain, but her charm warmed the room.

"Honey, these gentlemen are friends of Silky. This is my wife, Angela. Angela, this is Tony and Mark."

"Pleased to meet you, Angela," both Tony and I said.

"They are going to give me an opportunity to make some money. I'm going to be fencing clothes for them from the boosters. Will that be all right with you, baby?"

"Sure, sweetheart, we can use all of the money that we can get."

"Excuse me, gentlemen, but how are we going to set this thing up?"

I stepped in and said, "If all of the boosters could bring their merchandise here, then we would leave a big enough bank with you to buy out all designer merchandise at a third. You will then sell everything at half or better. We will take a third off of the top. The rest we will split down the middle with you."

Gerald's wife looked at Mark and her whole face lit up. She knew in her heart that all of their struggles would soon go away. She stepped closer to her man, putting her arms around his waist. She was looking up into his face waiting on him to say his next words.

"When would you like for me to start, Mark?" Gerald asked.

"Right now and I reached into my pocket and pulled out a roll of money, counted out five thousand dollars in hundred dollar bills. I then handed it to Gerald then said, "We want you to keep perfect records. How much you paid for everything, the total price of the merchandise and our profit. We will check with you every couple of days. And Silky, you can send all of the boosters here with their merchandise now. What we need for you to do is give us your phone number."

"Write down our phone number and give it to these gentlemen, honey."

Tony gave Gerald our business card and said, "If you have any problems, give us a call. We've got your back. Any questions, Gerald?"

"Just, thanks for giving me a chance to make some money. And I will do right by you guys."

"No, thank Silky, because he's the one that pulled our coat to you. And he spoke very highly of you. He has a lot of confidence in you that you will do a hell of a job with this merchandise thing. If Silky believes in you that much, then you are our man. All that we expect is for you to be honest and loyal to us. We believe that you will. With that we are going to have to go. We have some more stops to make. We'll see you in a couple of days."

On the way out, Gerald's wife said, "It was a pleasure meeting the both of you."

"It was a pleasure meeting you too, Angela."

And we all left the house and started across the street where Tony's Cadillac was parked. Tony unlocked the doors and we all got in.

Silky asked, "What do you think about Gerald?"

"I think that he is going to do well." I looked at Tony and he nodded in agreement. He started the engine and we slowly pulled off from the curb.

Chapter Fourteen

"The fencing business is going really good. Gerald has been with us for a few months now. He really has proven his worth."

"I've been doing a lot of thinking and we can take this thing to a whole new level. We can go legal with this."

Tony paused and looked at me strangely. "Mark, are you talking about going legal with the fencing business with Gerald?"

"Yeah, Tony, but it wouldn't be a fencing business. It would be a legitimate wholesale company."

"Break it down to me. Where are you going with this?'

"Okay, here it is. Years ago, before I met you, I knew this white guy that used to ride around in the black community selling merchandise out of the back of his van. He used to have some really nice women's outfits. At the time, I was pimpin' and I was always looking for a deal on designer outfits for my women. This guy had a little bit of everything. So I would buy from him occasionally. So would many other blacks. He would even go to small stores and sell to them at wholesale prices. I'd lost contact with this guy and it was a year before we connected again. And that's because he saw one of my girls working the street. He gave her a business card to give to me. Well, I looked past the phone numbers and read the address. I decided to go talk to him in person. And to my amazement, this guy had gone from a van to a huge warehouse selling merchandise. As I pulled up, I saw several eighteen-wheeler trucks parked at the loading docks. I walked into the warehouse and I saw all of these people walking around, shopping. I saw trucks being unloaded. I asked one of the men on the floor if Jake was in. The man said to follow him and we'd see. He led me to Jake's office. Jake was sitting behind a big oak desk. Jake looked at me as I walked into his office. 'Mark, my man, I'm glad that you came to see me. I see that your girl gave you my card.' Yeah, she said that you wanted me to call, I said, then asked if all of this was his? He told me it was—that it all belonged to him. In a year, he had really blown it up. I asked how he went from a van to a warehouse and he said that he started buying company close outs and overstocked merchandise below wholesale prices. He even bought distressed merchandise. He told me that the trick was to buy in half trucks and truckloads. The more you bought, the better the deal. He said that you start off small, with a pallet load or two. He asked if I was interested in starting my own business some day. I told him that the only business I was interested in was some good pimping. He laughed then took me on a tour of the place. He led me around his humongous warehouse. I was in a state of disbelief at how far this man had come in such a short period of time. At that time, I couldn't conceive me going into a legitimate business, but if I had known then what I know now, I would have."

"So after listening to your story, you're saying that that's what we should do?"

"That's right. That's what I'm saying. We need to step this thing up to a higher level."

"Okay, Mark, so where do we start?"

"We need to start by getting information on where to buy truckloads of merchandise. Then we need to find a place to store and sell our goods. We can sell our merchandise to small businesses and flea markets, street vendors. Anyone that wants to work for themselves will buy from us at wholesale prices."

Gerald is good with people and he has a way with them. He knows a little bit of everybody. I think that he will be good with keeping books as you can see with the fencing business. She can work with him as his secretary. I'm sure that they both will be thrilled to hold those positions."

"I like Gerald too, Mark. And he has been honest and very loyal. And he appreciated us getting him out of his financial difficulties. He will be the right man for that position."

"Okay then, Tony, let's put Joyce and Brenda on digging up the information on where to buy truckloads of merchandise of all types."

"By the way, Mark, did you buy anything that day when you were at Jake's warehouse?"

"Hell, yeah, man. I walked in with a bankroll that would choke an elephant, but after seeing all of that shit that he had, I just kept buying and buying! My ho's were happy as hell when they came home late that night and saw all of the things that I had bought. All I heard that night from those ho's was 'Thank you, Daddy, thank you, Daddy.' I said 'Yeah, let's see how joyous you ho's gone be tomorrow. I want you ho's out early humping your asses off getting my bank back right.'"

Tony started laughing.

I said, "So do you think that it's a good idea?"

"Sure, I think it's a great idea. My dream is for us to be all the way legitimate one day."

"I've been having the same dream myself, Tony."

"I think now is a good time for us to start thinking seriously about getting out of the drug business in Lansing. We have had a long run and we have made plenty of money. We've been very lucky. None of our main people have caught any cases. Eugene has been a good lieutenant and Dollar Bill, Curtis, Tommy and Margo have been good soldiers. All of them should have serious money. And if they just need to be busy, once we get this warehouse going here, we can open up another one in Lansing and let them run it, or they can start their own and buy from us."

"Man, you really do be coming up with some good ideas. I'll tell you what, Mark, once we get our warehouse going here, maybe we'll have Eugene and Curtis come down and see how it's set up and get an idea on how to run it down there."

"Cool, Tony, then we'll do that. We've put a lot on the table today. Joyce has my dinner waiting for me, so I'm going to go home and eat. She gets a little upset when I don't get home in time for dinner. If I didn't know better, I'd say that she's trying to get me fat, thinking that no other woman would want me."

Tony laughed. "That makes two of us. Brenda is doing the same thing."

"Okay, baby, I'll see you tomorrow." Then I got up and left.

When I got home, Joyce was waiting for me looking as beautiful as ever. She asked, "Are you hungry, sweetheart?"

"Yes, love, I'm starving. What did you cook?"

"I cooked some broiled steaks, smothered potatoes and onions, with green beans. Do you want me to fix your plate?"

"Yes, baby, please. I need to run upstairs for a moment. Plus I need to wash up." Then I stopped. "Oh, baby, tomorrow I need you to call Brenda. Tony and I had just got done kickin' it and we are going to start a new company."

"What type of company, sweetheart?"

"We are going to be selling all types of merchandise. From designer clothes to appliances. We are going to be buying our merchandise by the eighteen wheeler truckloads. We need you and Brenda to get a phone book and try to find out where we can buy truckloads of overstocked, close out and distressed merchandise. And get an *Entrepreneur* magazine and look through it."

Then I ran up the stairs and got ready for dinner. After dinner, we talked into the wee hours of the night about the new company.

A month later...September 15, 1977

Tony and I stopped by Gerald's house. He opened the door. He was excited as usual to see us. "Come in, come in and have a seat. Let me get the books and your money."

He came back with the books and the money and handed it to Tony. After looking over the books, he looked up at Gerald and said, "This is it! We are closing this business down!"

Gerald stood there for a moment with a confused look on his face and then said, "Tony, is there something wrong with the books?"

"No, no, the books are cool."

"Well, did I do something wrong?"

"Naw, you are alright. We'd like for you to take a ride with us."

"Alright. Let me go tell my wife," he said, still wearing a confused look on his face. Once he returned, we all left.

Twenty minutes into the ride, we were approaching the warehouse. I looked into my rearview mirror. Gerald was sitting there, looking as puzzled as ever. I pulled into this empty parking space in the lot next to the warehouse. We all exited the car and walked inside.

The look on Gerald's face was a look of amazement. I said, "This is where you and your wife will be working from now on. You will be the president and she will be the secretary. Are you alright with that?"

"You are damned right that I'm alright with it!" There was no more worry on Gerald's face. Only a look of happiness and joy.

"Thanks, Tony. Thanks, Mark. I must admit that I didn't know what was going on. Why didn't you guys tell me?"

"Because we wanted it to be a surprise, didn't we, Mark?" I nodded my head yes.

"Well, it certainly is one. Wait till I tell my wife. Does Silky know about this?"

"No, it will be a surprise to him as well."

"So when do I start, Mark?"

"You can start tomorrow. Here is your set of keys. And here is the alarm code written on this card. Come on, let's show you around so that you can see everything. But there is a lot more that you will have to order from the companies that we are going to be dealing with."

"Tomorrow we will have our women meet you here at 9 a.m. to help you with the basics. You will have to hire your own people. Our women will work with you and your wife for a couple of weeks helping you get set up."

We walked all around the warehouse. "So what do you think of the place?"

"I think that it's big as hell, Mark, and I love my office."

"Good, then, you should be happy here."

"Oh, I'm happy already. I just can't wait to see the look on Angela's face."

"Gerald, have you and Angela thought about having anymore children?"

"Well, we had talked about it, but we weren't doing so well financially. So we decided to hold off. If it wasn't for you and Tony, we might have lost our home. We owe so much to you both."

"No problem. We are glad that we found a good man to run things for us. Are you ready to go back home and break the news to your lovely wife?"

"Yes, Mark, I'm ready."

We all left. We dropped Gerald off at home. Now, Tony and I were wishing that we had gone in with Gerald just to see the look on his wife's face when he told her the good news.

Chapter Fifteen

February 20, 1978...

It was a new year and everything was beautiful. It seemed like nothing could go wrong. Everything that we touched seemed to turn to gold. The merchandise company was doing very well. We were seeing a huge profit.

Gerald had a full staff working for him. Large shipments were coming in and he was moving them out just as fast. He had sharp business skills, he knew how to bring in new customers. We had many merchants buying their supplies from us. We sold some of everything, from designer clothes to appliances.

Things were going very well for Tony and me. The jewelry store and the diamond wholesale company and now, the warehouse full of all types of merchandise.

Joy and Renee have been in Atlanta now since September of 1977. They both loved it here. We had bought both of the girls a condominium in the same building.

We decided to let them work in the warehouse. They were both thrilled to be doing something. I had bought Joy a brand new red Thunderbird with white upholstery. Wouldn't you know that Tony bought Renee a brand new Thunderbird as well. Canary yellow with black interior.

Our man, Mr. Davis, that runs our jewelry store and diamond wholesale company suggested that this would be a good time to open up our second M&J Rare Jewelers store. We agreed. I told him to find the right location and to go ahead with it.

Tony, Renee, Joy and I joined a fitness center. We go and work out for an hour a day, five days a week.

Four days later...on February the 24th

I was sitting at home spending a quiet evening with Joyce. Suddenly my phone rang. I picked it up. "Hello."

"Hello, Mark. This is Attorney Goodman."

"How are you doing, Mr. Goodman?"

"I am doing fine, but I'm afraid that I have some bad news for you."

"What is it, sir?"

"I got a phone call from Eugene about an hour ago. He said that he, William, Tommy, Curtis and Margo are all in jail."

"All of them are in jail?" I asked.

"That's right, Mark. All of them. The Lansing, Michigan grand jury had indicted them all on charges that they sold large quantities of heroin. All but Margo and Eugene. Margo is charged with money laundering and Eugene is charged with conspiracy. Now if you want my office to represent them, I believe that I can get Margo and Eugene off fairly easy, because with the money laundering, I understand that they found three hundred ninety thousand dollars in Margo's house. Those bastards want that money and if they don't have to fight for it, they might be willing to drop the charges.

"Now I don't know all of the details and I won't know until the courts open up on Monday when they all go for their arraignment and be formally charged. They will all get bonds at that time. So you tell me what you want to do?"

"Well, Mr. Goodman, I want you and your firm to handle this."

"Okay, Mark, if that's what you want, then that's what we'll do. We will get on it first thing Monday morning. Now what are you going to do about their bail?"

"I'm going to fly in. I'll probably be leaving Sunday night. So, is everybody else charged with trafficking heroin?"

"That is correct, Mark, one count each and engaging in a pattern of corrupt activities. All but Eugene and Margo. Margo with the money laundering."

"So what you are saying is that the case doesn't look too strong against Eugene?"

"I don't think so. But let me look into it Monday. I'll have more information then."

"Very well, Mr. Goodman."

"Oh, yeah, Mark, how is your and Tony's business going?"

"It's going great, Mr. Goodman. Our diamond wholesale company is doing good. And our jewelry store is doing wonderful as well. We are actually getting ready to open up our second jewelry store. We just opened up a merchandise company about six or seven months ago and it's making money. Tony and I were just talking a week ago about how beautiful things were going for us and how it seemed like nothing could go wrong. I guess we couldn't foresee the future."

"Well, Mark, things happen, and when they do, we just have to be prepared for them. Don't get stressed out. Let my colleagues and me do all of the stressing. Like I said, I believe that we can win the first half of the battle fairly easy. It's the second half that's unknown."

"Listen, give my regards to Tony. Is he going to be coming with you?"

"No, one of us has to stay here and keep an eye on things. I'll be coming by myself."

"Alright, Mark. Then I'll talk to you when I see you."

"See you Monday, Mr. Goodman." We both hung up.

I sat there with my head in my hands. Thinking. Is this shit falling apart? I picked up the phone to call Tony. Brenda answered.

"Hello, Brenda."

"Hi, Mark."

"Is your man in?"

"Yes, hold on. Let me get him."

"Hello."

"Hey, Tony, got some bad news, man."

"What is it?"

"Mr. Goodman just called. Everyone is in jail. I'm talking about everyone, including Margo. They knocked her with three hundred ninety thousand cash. Eugene, they got him for conspiracy. Everyone else was hit with one count of trafficking and engaging in a pattern of corrupt activities."

"Goddamn, man! They got everybody!"

"Yeah, it's time for us to get out of the game like we talked about, Tony. We don't need to, and they don't need to go through this kinda shit no more. We all have made a decent living. And as you can see, we have stayed in this shit too long. I'm going to fly down on Sunday where I can be there Monday morning and raise everyone on bail. Once everyone is out, we'll work with the cases then. Mr. Goodman's firm is going to handle everything."

"Good, Mark, I'm going to fly down with you."

"No, baby, you stay here and keep an eye on things. It don't take both of us to handle this."

"Are you taking Joyce with you, Mark?"

"No, I'm going alone."

"Make sure that you take a warm coat with you because you know that the winters are bitter cold in Lansing."

"I will. Listen, what are you and Brenda doing tomorrow?"

"Well, we don't have anything planned for tomorrow. What do you have in mind?"

"I was thinking that you guys can come over and have dinner with Joyce and me. And maybe watch some movies afterwards. Since Sunday I'm leaving and Saturday is my last day here, I thought that we could spend it together."

"Hey, Mark, we'll be there. What time do you want us to come?"

"Come about 4 o'clock. We'll eat dinner about 5."

"Cool, I'll see you tomorrow."

"Okay, Tony, tomorrow it is. I'll talk to you then," I said hanging up the phone.

The following day, we enjoyed a lovely dinner and watched a couple of movies. The next day I had to leave.

I had just arrived in Detroit's Metropolitan Airport. I was on my way to pick up my rental car. As I stepped out of the car rental place, the frigid cold hit me in the face. I was glad that I had taken Tony's good advice and I brought a big heavy coat with me.

I drove to Lansing and checked into the Capitol Park Hotel. I took a nice hot shower, ordered room service and kicked back onto the bed, waiting for my food to arrive.

I decided that it was a good time to call Tony and let him know that I had arrived safely. I picked up the phone and dialed his number. After a few rings, he answered the phone. "Hello."

"Tony, I was just calling to let you know that I had made it in safely."

"That's good, Mark. How long have you been there?"

"I've been here a little over an hour. I had just taken my shower and now I'm waiting on room service to bring my dinner."

"What did you order for dinner?"

"Just some chicken fingers, French fries and a coke."

"I see that you and I both like those chicken fingers."

"Yeah, man, they are really good. I enjoy them."

"So what type of dessert are you getting?"

"What makes you think that I'm getting dessert, Tony?"

"Because I know you. You love your sweets."

"You're right. I'm getting some German chocolate cake and a scoop of vanilla ice cream. Man, you were right about bringing a heavy coat because it's colder than a well digger's ass in Montana here."

"I told you."

"Yeah, you did and I took your advice. Someone is knocking at my door. Hold on for a moment. I think that's room service."

I opened the door. The waiter came in with the tray of food. He sat the tray on the table and handed me my bill. I paid him and gave him a five dollar tip. He said, "Thank you, sir," with a smile, then asked if there was anything else that I needed.

"No, thank you, that will be all for this evening," and I let him out.

I picked up the phone. "Tony, I'm back."

"What time are you going to be in court tomorrow?"

"Well, you know that court starts at 9 o'clock in the morning. I'll get there early because I want to meet with the attorneys before court."

"That's a good idea, Mark. So are you going to call me after court?"

"Yeah, I'll call you as soon as I get back from court. And if everything goes right, everyone should be out."

"Okay, then, I'll talk to you tomorrow. Go ahead and finish eating your dinner before it gets cold."

"Yeah, later, Tony," and we hung up.

Monday morning at 8 a.m....

I met with my attorneys in their office. We went over the formalities. Mr. Goodman was explaining to me that they are going to go in front of the judge. At that time the judge will read off the charges, and they will enter a plea of not guilty on all of their behalf. The judge will then set bond for all of them. Now, Mark, I took it upon myself to call the bondsman and told him to be at the courthouse and be ready to bail everyone out for you. He said that he would be there because you and Tony always take care of your business."

I then handed Mr. Goodman a brown paper bag and told him that there was fifty thousand dollars in it. I asked him if he would like to count it before we left?

"No need to Mark. I think that we'd better get going."

We arrived at the courthouse at a quarter to nine. Their office was only four blocks away, so we decided to walk.

I don't know how these white guys do it. They act like this freezing weather didn't bother them. I was freezing my ass off. Even my dick was cold.

When we arrived at the courthouse, the bondsman was standing in the hallway. He saw us walking up and smiled. "Mark, it's good to see you again." We shook hands.

"Same to you, Mr. Richardson."

"Well, as soon as they give them a bond, we'll get them right out."

Mr. Goodman said, "Let's go into the courtroom and get this ball rolling."

As we walked into the courtroom, my lawyer and the bondsman walked to the front. I took a seat in the back. Mr. Richardson took a seat in the front row. My lawyer opened a little swinging gate and took a seat at the attorney's table.

A few moments later, the bailiff said, "Everybody rise." As the judge was walking to his bench, he said, "The Honorable Judge Fisher presiding."

The judge then sat down and said, "You may be seated now."

The first case up was ours. They brought Eugene, Tommy, William, Curtis and Margo out. The proceedings were brief. The judge read their charges and accepted their pleas, gave them bonds and set their court date for March 26th, a month later. I waited around the courthouse for about an hour. Everyone was released.

We all stopped by Margo's house. I wanted to run down what Tony and my plans were to them. I said, "Everyone have a seat. This is what's happening. Some of you are going to do some time. And some of you won't. The thing is, getting it down to as less time as possible. I've talked to Mr. Goodman and to Mr. Goldstein. They are both going to be representing you all.

"Margo, the case against you and Eugene, the lawyers feel confident that they will be dismissed, in time. The three hundred ninety thousand dollars, we are going to have to forfeit it. As long as we don't put up a fight, they will drop the charges.

"Now, Eugene, the only thing that they have on you is that they've seen you going to a couple of our houses a few times. So this conspiracy shit is weak as well. They just want to lock everyone up. See, they've always known who we were. They just couldn't build a case against us. Tony and I have been doing some big things since we've been in Atlanta, and we have been doing a lot of talking about going all the way legitimate. You guys have been friends of Tony's for many years. Now you all have been friends of mine for the last seven years. We are done with the drug business."

"Excuse me, Mark, but just because we all got busted, you are closing everything down for good?" Eugene asked.

"Yeah, man, we don't have to close down. We could just move our spots," Dollar Bill said.

"Yeah, I'm not worried about doing no time. I knew what I was up against when I got into this shit," said Curtis.

Margo sat silently with her hands clenched between her thighs.

"Is there something that you want to say, Margo?"

"No, Mark, whatever decision that you and Tony make is alright with me. I know that you guys only want the best for us. I know where you are going with this. You don't want to see us going in and out of prisons."

"That's right, baby girl. You hit it on the head. Listen up everybody. This is what we were talking about. We have just opened up a merchandise business in a large warehouse in Atlanta. We sell some of everything from clothes to appliances. You name it, we have it. We sell to all of the merchants. Maybe not all of the merchants, but we have our share. And it's a large share. We have a diamond wholesale company. Two jewelry stores called M&J Rare Jewelers.

"Now what we want to do is to open up another merchandise warehouse here in Lansing. And maybe bring Eugene and Curtis down to Atlanta so that they can learn to run a business of that magnitude. You guys can run that business here and make handsome salaries. Or you can own the business yourselves and buy your supplies from Tony and me.

"What I'm saying here is that you all have made decent money. And you don't need to make a career out of being a drug dealer. What I'm about to say next may shock you, but it's true. We can't continue poisoning our people with this garbage. It's time for us to give something back to our community and the children of the community. I know that some of you may be sitting there saying to yourself that this is not the Mark that we knew. You are right. I have grown over the years. I see things now in ways that I've never seen them before. So what do you all think about our proposal?"

Margo jumped straight up and said, "I'm all for it, Mark! And if you don't mind, I would like to move to Atlanta and work at the warehouse there once all of this is over."

"If that's what you want, baby girl, then I'll get you a place."

"That's what I want, Mark. I'm ready to leave this town. Plus, I miss you and Tony."

"Alright. What about the rest of you all?"

Eugene said, "Hell, it sounds good to me."

"Me too," Curtis said.

Dollar Bill said, "I don't want to be no career criminal."

Tommy said, "Let's do this thing. I could be a boss."

I said, "You all will be bosses. You will be hiring all of your people yourselves. Now do you want to work for me and Tony or do you want to own the place yourselves?"

Eugene stood up and said, "I think that we'd like to own it ourselves. What about it, fellows?"

Everyone nodded his head in agreement.

"But we need to come to Atlanta and learn how to run it," Curtis said.

"No problem. When I call Tony tonight, he is really going to be proud of your decision. Are there any questions? If not, I am going back to my hotel room and get some rest. I am going back to Atlanta in a couple of days."

"There are no questions, Mark."

Everybody spoke up in agreement.

I then stood up and kissed Margo. I shook everyone else's hand, then I left for my hotel room to call Tony.

Once I got into my room, I took off my coat and sat down on the bed. I picked up the phone to dial Tony. The phone rang. Moments later, he answered.

"Hello."

"Hey, Tony, what's up? This is Mark. Everybody is out."

"That's good, Mark. When is their next court date?"

"March 26th. I ran everything down to them about what we had discussed about opening up a merchandise warehouse down here in Lansing. They didn't like the idea about us getting out of the drug business, but I told them that we weren't trying to make a career out of it and that you and I are trying to do bigger and better tings and wanted them to be a part of it.

"Once I explained it all to them, they all agreed. They said that they wanted to be their own bosses. I agreed to bring Eugene and Curtis down to the warehouse here to learn how to set up and run their business. I told them that they could purchase all of their merchandise from us. Margo asked if she could move to Atlanta and work in our warehouse. I told her that it would be cool. That we would love to have her here with us. So what do you think, Tony?"

"So are you asking me what I think about Margo moving here?"

"That, and the fellows' decision."

"Well, I think it's good that Margo wants to move here. She's sure welcome too. And as far as the fellows' decision, that's what I wanted anyway. You can only go so far with this thing before something goes wrong. As you can see with the cases that everyone has now. They all have paper and no one is hurting. And with the merchandise company, they will have security."

"Okay then, Tony. I just wanted to give you a rundown on everything that went on today. I'm going to go and chill out now. I'll be back the day after tomorrow."

"Okay, I'll see you then, Mark."

"Alright, I'll see you." I hung up and laid back on my bed.

Chapter Sixteen

August 15, 1978...

The time has gone past so quickly. The prosecutors made deals with all of our people. They dropped all charges against Margo and Eugene.

Our attorneys did a wonderful job getting Curtis, Tommy and Dollar Bill's charges reduced. Each one was facing seven to twenty-five years. But the lawyers were able to get them down to two to ten years. All should be out within eighteen months.

Margo and Eugene both came to Atlanta. Eugene is just there to learn the business. When everyone else gets out, they are going to start their new company.

Margo is here to stay. She is now working at the warehouse with Joy and Renee and loving it. We bought Margo a condominium in the same building that Joy and Renee live in. She's dating a guy that lives on the floor above her.

Tony and I have both met him a few times. He seems to be a decent guy. As long as she's happy, we are cool with it.

I decided to make my rounds. I stopped at the jewelry store. As I walked in, I saw Silky standing at the counter looking at one of our beautiful diamond rings. I walked up on him without him even knowing that I was there. I said to him in a hard tone, "Don't move, buddy, don't even think about it!"

He dropped the ring on the counter and turned and saw that it was me. "Goddamn, Mark! You just about made me shit on myself!" he said.

"We wouldn't want that. Your ho's coming home smelling like fish, and here you are smelling like shit. Damn, it's good to see you, Silky. How have you been?"

"I'm doing good, baby. But next time, don't sneak up on me like that. I can't take that shit. The way that I be knocking these nigga's ho's, ain't no telling who wants to do something to me."

"Damn, baby. You got my man Gerald as happy as a sissy in Boys Town. And that's happy. A sissy in Boys Town around all of them boys. You know that he's happy."

"Yeah, Silky, Gerald is a good man. We are glad that you introduced us to him. He did so well for us in the fencing business, that we decided to step it up to a legal level."

"He likes his position as president," Silky said. "And his wife is happy as hell. Every time that I see him, he can't say enough about you and Tony. This guy loves the both of you."

"We like him. I see you buying yourself a new ring." I had to give my man some play.

"Can I get a finder's discount, Mark?"

"A finder's discount. What did you find?"

"I found Gerald for you."

"Jackie, what's the ticket on that ring?"

"Mr. Jones, it's three thousand four hundred and ninety-nine dollars."

"Okay." I thought for a moment. "Knock the four hundred ninety-nine off."

"Thanks, Mark." Silky leaned over and said in a low voice, "I like the way that she said Mr. Jones."

"I demand that all of my employees be professional. This is my business and I take it very serious, Silky."

"You and Tony are two smooth young brothers."

"Thanks, baby. Is there anything else that I can do for you before I leave?"

"No, Mark, I'm going to browse around and see if I can find something for my bottom ho. She has really been making me a lot of paper lately. And she just beat a sucker the other night out of three grand."

"So how many ho's do you have now?"

"I had ten, but I only have nine now. One ran off a few nights ago. She's a renegade."

"Have you ever thought about getting out of the game?"

"And do what, Mark? This is what I live for. I don't know how to do anything but pimp. It's pimp or die for me, baby!"

"If you ever decide to get out, and you have a little money saved up, maybe I can help you go into some kind of business for yourself."

"Yeah, maybe I can get a ho house or something, Mark."

"Well, Silky. That's not what I had in mind. Anyway, baby, just think about it. I've got to go."

I left the store and stopped by Joy's condominium. When I walked through the door, Joy, Margo and Renee were all sitting around talking. Joy ran up to me and gave me a hug and a kiss and said, "Hi, baby, how was your day?"

Margo got up and hugged and kissed me as well.

"Alright now, Margo," Joy playfully said.

"Girl, that's my big brother," Margo said.

"Hi, Mark," Renee said.

"Hi, Renee, ain't none of you girls working today or what?"

"Sweetheart, we are working, but we are on our lunch break."

I glanced at my watch. "Oh, I'm sorry. I didn't notice what time it was."

"Sweetheart, can I speak to you for a moment in private, please?"

"Sure, baby, is there something wrong?"

"No, I just need to talk to you about something. Would y'all excuse us for a minute?"

"Yeah, girl, go ahead," Renee said.

Joy and I walked into the bedroom. Once inside, she said, "Baby, sit down for a minute."

I sat on the bed and she sat next to me.

"What is it, baby?" I asked, looking into her beautiful brown eyes.

"Baby, I was just wondering if I could go down to Lansing and visit my family for about a week?"

"Sure you can, sweetheart. When would you like to leave?"

"I was thinking in a few days, if that's alright?"

"Sure, baby. That would be fine. Why don't you go shopping for something for your whole family. Get them all a nice gift from the both of us."

"I will, baby, they will like that," Joy smiled.

"Would you like for me to go with you, sweetheart?"

"No, honey, you've been doing a lot of traveling lately. And Tony needs you here to help out."

"Are you sure, 'cause I will drop everything for you."

"Yes, baby. I'm sure. I'll be okay."

"Baby, you call me when you get there."

"I'll call you everyday when I'm there. But I'm not leaving for a few days."

"Well, Joy, when you get off of work tonight, I'll be back and spend the night with you."

"Alright, baby, I'm going to fix dinner for us tonight."

"That will be nice, Joy."

Later that evening, I stopped back at Joy's house. Dinner was ready. We have a lovely dinner. It was good to spend some quality time with Joy. I enjoyed it so much that I told her that I would spend every minute with her until she left for Lansing.

We never left the house. We talked. We laughed. We made love. It was everything that I should have been doing more of. I needed the break from everything. I called Tony and told him that it was on him for the next few days and if he needed me for anything, I would be here with my Joy.

"Naw, baby, stay there and relax. You need a break. I can handle everything," Tony said.

"Thanks, man. She needs me and I need to be here with her. You understand."

"Everything that's understood need not be explained."

"Thanks again, Tony. Talk to you later." At that time we both hung up the phone.

Three days later...Lansing, Michigan

It was a hot day in August. Joy had been back in Lansing for a couple of days now. She borrowed her mother's '88 Oldsmobile. She told her mother that she had wanted to go out and see some of her old friends.

Her mother told her that some of her old friends had been stopping by from time to time asking about her since she'd been living in Atlanta.

She told her mother, "I'll be back in a few hours." Her mother told her to go out and enjoy the weather, to have a good time. Joy drove down Washinaw Street and turned right onto Logan. A few blocks down the street she stopped for a red light. As she waited on the light, someone called her name. She looked over to her left. It was Betty coming out of Calhoun's Restaurant.

Joy yelled back, "Hold on, girl," and turned the corner.

Betty walked over to the car. "How long have you been back home? Is Mark with you?" Betty asked.

"I've been back a few days now, but I came alone. Mark is still in Atlanta."

"I stopped by your mother's house a few times asking about you. You know that I'm a lawyer now. I'm working for the prosecutor's office downtown."

"No, girl. I didn't know. Mark is going to be proud of you. He always says that he's seen a lot of people in the ghetto doing the wrong things, but he said that you are one that will make a difference. Mark is really crazy about you. And very proud of you. I can't wait to tell him that our Betty is a lawyer."

Betty blushed. "Well, Joy, I've got to run now. Let me give you my card before I go. If there is ever anything that I can do for you or Mark, don't hesitate to give me a call. If it wasn't for Mark, none of this would have happened. The money that he gave me and my mother after my father passed away made it all possible."

"Betty, I'll be sure to tell Mark that I saw you."

"Alright, girl, you take care. I'm going to stop by and holler at you before you go back to Atlanta."

"Alright. Bye, Betty, but be sure to stop by and holler."

"Bye, Joy. Take care. I will."

Betty walked away from the car and Joy pulled off. Joy decided to stop at the mall. Once inside, she was just enjoying herself, stopping at one store and then another. She was on her way into the men's store to purchase something for her father and her little brother when she noticed Frank. "Hi, Frank!"

"Joy, how long have y'all been back?"

"I came alone. Mark is still in Atlanta. Where is Karen?"

"She's somewhere around here, spending my money. What are you looking for, something slick for Mark?"

"No, I was looking for something for my father and my little brother. They both like to dress sharp."

"Well, it was nice seeing you, Joy. Tell Mark that I said hi when you talk to him. Maybe Karen and I will run into you again before you leave. I hope you find something nice."

"Thanks. I'll see you later, Frank. And if by chance I don't run into you before I leave, you guys stop by and holler at me. I'll be going back to Atlanta in four or five days, so tell Karen to stop by."

"So where are you staying while you're here?" Frank asked while scanning the mall looking for any sign of Karen.

"I'm staying at my mother's house."

"If we don't see you before we leave the mall, then we'll stop by there."

They both said their goodbyes and parted. Joy went into the store and purchased a few items for her father and little brother, then went on to purchase something for her mother and little sister. Then she headed home.

Two days later...

That evening, Joy decided to drive around on Butler Street. It was very warm that night and the streets were packed. People were everywhere. Joy parked her car and walked up to the bar-b-que joint where many of her friends were standing out on the porch. They were all glad to see her. She received many hugs and kisses. Jean, a young beautiful woman with wide hips and large breasts that Joy had gone to school with walked up and gave Joy a hug. "I'd heard that you were back in town, but I didn't know where you were staying."

"I'm staying at my mother's house. You know that she is not going to let me stay anywhere else!"

"I started to come over to your mother's house and I would have eventually. Joy, you really look good. How's Mark doing?"

"He's doing good. Just staying busy with all of the companies that we have."

"With all of the companies? How many companies do y'all have, girl?"

"Well, we own two jewelry stores and a diamond wholesale business. And we have a warehouse where we sell all kinds of merchandise to many of the merchants in the city of Atlanta and the surrounding area. We have been thinking about putting a warehouse here in Lansing."

"Now that would be really nice. We need something like that around here for black people, Joy."

"I know, and Mark and Tony are really thinking about putting one here. Eugene, Dollar Bill, Tommy and Curtis will be running it. They may even be the owners and buy their supplies from Mark and Tony. I'm not sure which way they are going to go with it, but my understanding is that it's going to happen."

"Girl, I hope that I can get a job there. I sure could use one."

"Well, when it opens, talk to Eugene. Tell Eugene that you've talked to me about a job in the warehouse and to call my man to verify it. I'll talk to Mark when I get back to Atlanta and tell him that we've talked."

"Joy, do you think Mark will okay it?"

"That's my baby. He'll do that for me."

"Thanks, girl."

"You're welcome. It sure is a lot of people out here tonight."

"Joy, you know when it gets warm out, our people are going to come out in vast numbers. It's always been like that. Ain't nothing changed since you and Mark been gone. It might be more people out now than when you were living here, but everything is still about the same."

"Well, it's certainly warm out here tonight and I can understand people wanting to get out of the house. Listen, Jean, I'd love to stand here and talk longer, but my family is waiting on these good ribs so I'd better go on in here and get them so I can get back home. Stop by tomorrow and holler at me if you get a chance because I'll be leaving the day after."

"I will, I promise."

Joy went in and ordered two slabs of ribs. And boy, did they smell good. She paid for the ribs and walked out the door.

As Joy was walking towards the car there were two guys standing in front of it. As she continued walking toward her car, Butch asked Leo, "Ain't that Mark's bitch, Joy?"

"Yeah, that's her," Leo said, "why?"

"Her old man had something to do with them killing my uncle. We are going to have some fun with this bitch tonight," Butch said as he grabbed his dick.

"I'm with that!" laughed Leo.

As Joy was ready to pass the men that were standing there, Butch said, "Joy, what's up?"

Joy stopped, but she didn't recognize him as anyone that she knew.

"Where is my man, Mark?"

"Oh, Mark is still in Atlanta. Do I know you all?"

"No, but your man Mark knows us. I'm Butch and this is Leo," he said as they walked up on Joy.

"I'll tell Mark that you both said hello."

At that time, Butch pulled out his .38 special and shoved it into her ribs. "No, you tell that punk to fuck himself! Now get your black ass into this car, bitch, and you better not scream or I'll kill your ass!"

Joy's whole body was shaking something terrible. She climbed into the car with them. They sat on each side of her while Leo drove off.

As they were pulling past the bar-b-que joint, Jean, Joy's friend, was standing on the sidewalk. She looked and noticed that Joy sat between Butch and Leo with a look of terror on her face. She had heard the rumors that Mark may have had something to do with Slim getting killed. And she knew that Butch was Slim's nephew and feared for Joy's safety.

Jean decided to immediately go and tell Joy's mother what she'd seen.

Later, back at the house...

The two men that had snatched Joy pulled up around the back of Butch's house. They made Joy ride on the floor up under the dash. Once parked, they exited the vehicle pulling Joy by the hair. "Come on, bitch." They entered the house and immediately went into the bedroom. Butch said to Joy, "You're going to be a very busy bitch tonight. Take off your clothes, bitch. Everything. And I mean everything!"

Joy was standing there shaking with fear. A feeling that she had never experienced before in her life. She was terrified. She pleaded with the men. "Please, don't. Don't hurt me. What have I done to you all?"

"Bitch, it's not what you did, it's what your man did to my uncle. Now get those clothes off." Butch then hit her so hard that she saw stars. As Joy fell to the floor, she was crying and shaking so bad. Finally, she got up off the floor taking everything off as the man had ordered.

Joy stood in front of both men. Naked. Butch ordered her to turn around so that they could admire her beautiful body.

"Damn, this is one beautiful bitch!" Leo said. Then Butch said, "Bend over, bitch. Spread your ass cheeks. Let me see where I'm going to be entering at."

Joy complied. She bent over and took her hands and spread her ass cheeks.

Butch said, "Oh, yeah, I'm going to love fucking this tight, fine asshole."

Joy shook even more.

"My friend only likes head and pussy. So you've got it easy there, bitch."

Then Leo said, "Yeah, that's what I like. I hope that you can suck a dick good. Can you do that?"

Joy stood there staring at the men, pleading with her eyes. If only Mark was here!

At that moment, Butch started beating her like a man. He hit her so hard that it cut the top of her eye. Blood shot everywhere. She screamed out in pain.

Leo shouted, "Hey, man, don't fuck her up where she can't do nothing. I want a good blow job from this bitch."

Butch took off his belt and started whipping Joy. He must have beat her for at least five minutes. And all the time he was talking to her saying, "You are going to be a good little sex slave, aren't you? You are going to do everything that we tell you to do, aren't you, little bitch?"

"Yes, yes, just stop beating me," she cried out.

"Get in bed, bitch," Butch ordered.

She jumped up with lightning speed and got into the bed, shaking something fierce.

Butch looked at Leo. He winked his eye and smiled. "I think that we've got a good little bitch here. Get undressed and let's have some fun."

Once the men were completely naked, Joy was looking at both of them, but what terrified her most was the size of Butch. He must have been twelve inches and very thick. She cried that much more!

Butch said, "Bitch, look how lucky you are. You get to take all of this dick up your sweet little ass."

Joy opened her mouth, attempting to plead with him. He placed a finger to her lips and said, "Hush, you're going to enjoy this."

Chapter Seventeen

Joy's mother had just opened the door for Jean. "Hi, Jean, Joy's not at home right now."

"I know, Mrs. Reed. I just saw her on Butler Street and I think that something bad is going to happen."

"What makes you think something like that, Jean?"

"I saw her pull off in a car with two guys and she looked terrified. And these are not very nice guys."

Mrs. Reed stepped back. "Come on in," she said with a look of worry on her face.

Jean came in and asked Mrs. Reed, "Can you get in touch with Mark? Please, would you call him? I need to talk to him. I don't feel good about this."

"What do you think is going to happen to my daughter?"

"I don't know, Mrs. Reed, I don't know."

Joy's mother grabbed her phone book. She peeled through the pages. Once she located Mark's number, she began to dial, fearing for her daughter.

When the phone rang, Mark was getting ready to leave. He answered the phone. "Hello."

"Mark, this is Joy's mother."

"Oh, hi, Mrs. Reed. How are you doing?"

"I'm fine, but I'm afraid that something might have happened to Joy."

"What do you mean, Mrs. Reed, something might have happened to Joy? I don't understand!"

"Her friend, Jean, is sitting here," she said. "Here, let me put her on. She can tell you herself."

"Hello, Mark, this is Jean. I was around on Butler Street. Joy and I were just talking then she went inside to get some ribs. She came out and was walking to her car. The next thing that I noticed, she was in a car with Slim's nephew Butch and his friend Leo. She had a terrified look on her face as they drove down the street, as if something was wrong!"

"How long has it been since it happened?"

"About thirty minutes, more or less."

"Jean, can you get in touch with my man, Eugene? Tell him that I said to get out in the streets and find Joy. Tell him to pay anybody that has any information. Now put Mrs. Reed back on the phone."

"Mark, what do you think is going on?"

"I don't know, Mrs. Reed. Don't worry. I'm going to get a flight out of here tonight. I'll get there as fast as I can."

"Mark, maybe I should call the police."

"No, just wait. She may come home before I get there. If not, I'll find her when I get there, I promise."

"Okay, sweety. But please hurry, Mark."

"I will. Bye, Mrs. Reed," and I hung up.

Forty-five minutes later...

Butch told Leo, "You lay down on the bed and open your legs. Bitch, you get between his legs."

Joy immediately complied with his order. Butch grabbed a jar of Vaseline from off of the dresser and handed it to her. "You know what to do with this, bitch, grease me up."

Joy took some of the grease and stroked it up and down over every inch of Butch's huge dick as her tears flowed down her face. Butch took the jar from her. He put a finger in the grease and pulled it out, covered with Vaseline. "Bitch, bend over and spread your ass cheeks wide!"

When she bent down, her head bumped Leo's dick. Leo smiled and said, "Bitch, while you are down here, put this dick in your mouth and suck it!" Joy complied. "Damn, this bitch got some good hot head," he laughed.

Butch said, "I hope that her asshole is just as good," and he rammed his finger full of grease up her ass. Then he positioned himself.

As he plunged himself into her, she screamed out in agony. "Oh, God." And it seemed to bring more pleasure to Butch. He had no mercy on her. He split her ass wide open. Blood spilled from her ass as he plunged deeper and deeper inside of her.

She passed out from pain, as he came inside of her. His eyes rolled up in back of his head from the pleasure that he felt from this virgin asshole. He loved it, and he loved inflicting pain on her.

As he pulled out, her bowels broke as well. But that didn't stop them from continuing to have their way with her for the rest of the night.

Around five the next morning, they finished with her. They dropped her off by her car. She was bleeding profusely, barely able to crawl back into the car. She drove herself to Lansing General Hospital, where she had to have immediate surgery. He had ruptured her insides. The hospital notified her family and they were all waiting on her to come out of surgery. Her little brother remained at the house waiting on Mark to arrive.

My plane had just arrived at Detroit Metropolitan Airport. Joyce had dropped me off at the airport in Atlanta. She was wondering why I had to leave in such a hurry. I told her that there was some unexpected business that came up and to call Tony later that day and let him know that I was on my way to Lansing.

I walked out of the terminal and got on the shuttle to take me to pick up my car rental. After I got my rental, I drove to Lansing. I arrived in Lansing and was at Joy's mother's house within an hour. Her little brother answered the door and said, "Everybody is at the hospital. They left me here to wait on you."

"At the hospital! At the hospital for what?"

"Joy is in the hospital. They took her up for surgery."

"Surgery!" I was extremely upset. "Come on, let's go!"

At the hospital, I stopped at the nurse's station and asked what room Joy Reed was in.

"Are you a family member?" asked the receptionist without looking up from reading through her files.

"Yes, I'm her husband and this is her brother."

"She's in room 448. Take the elevator on the left to the fourth floor." She handed me two passes and we headed for the elevator.

Once in the room, Joy's whole family was sitting around. Mrs. Reed's eyes were red and swollen. Joy's little sister's eyes were also red and swollen. They had been crying all night.

I asked Joy's mother, "What happened to Joy?"

"Mark, Joy has been beaten real bad. She was violated and sodomized and she lost a lot of blood. They had ruptured her insides. She was rushed immediately into surgery. The doctors had just left saying that the surgery had gone well and she's in the recovery room now. And once the anesthesia wears off, they will bring her to the room.

"Excuse me, Mrs. Reed. I have to step out and make a phone call. I'll be right back." I went to the phone in the hallway. I called Eugene and asked him if he heard anything. I was mad as hell. I wanted to kill someone. He said that he knows where Butch lives and that he has been going past there keeping an eye on the house. I told him not to make a move until I get with him. He asked where I was.

"I'm still at the hospital waiting for my woman to come down from the recovery room. I'm going to punish these guys, Eugene. And I mean punish them. They are going to beg for me to kill them.

"Listen, I've got to get back to the room. Keep an eye out for those bastards. I'll talk to you later." I then hung up.

After being back in the room for a few moments, they wheeled Joy in and carefully lifted her into the bed.

Mrs. Reed leaned over and gently touched Joy's face. "Robert, look what they've done to our baby." Tears started rolling down her face from her red swollen eyes once again.

"I hope that they catch those bastards and prosecute them to the fullest extent of the law. How could any man do this to a woman?" he screamed out. "Hell, they're not men, they're fuckin' animals! That's what they are, fuckin' animals!"

"Robert, calm down. You are getting too loud. This is a hospital. They will put us out," said Mrs. Reed as she tried to calm her husband.

"I'm sorry, I can't help it, honey, look what they did to our baby." Robert sat in the chair and put his head in his hands and sobbed.

All this time, I was standing by the bed letting Joy's parents express their emotions. At the same time, my heart was heavy. I wanted revenge for what they did to my woman. I put her hand into mine and leaned over and kissed her gently on her forehead. I'm not sure if she could see me, because her face was so badly swollen. She spoke to me in a weak voice, "Mark, I love you, baby. I'm sorry, Mark. Please forgive me."

"You did nothing wrong, sweetheart. You did nothing wrong. I shouldn't have let you come by yourself. Tell me, did Butch and his friend do this to you?"

"Please, Mark, I don't want anything bad to happen to you."

"There is nothing going to happen to me, baby. Just answer the question."

Joy was silent for a moment. "Yes. Yes, baby, they hurt me real bad. They made me do things. I'm sorry. I had to. They beat me. They beat me so bad. They beat me with their fists, then they beat me with a belt. I was scared to death. I thought that they were going to kill me. I didn't want to do all of those sick things. Will you still love me, baby?" she whispered in a low voice.

I had to keep my ear close to her so that I could hear every word that she was saying. I was holding one of her hands and I placed my other hand gently on the side of her face. I kissed her lips softly and said, "I will always love you, baby. You are my Joy!"

For three days, I never left the room. When her family would come to see her, her mother would always bring something for me to eat. I hadn't changed clothes in three days. I would go into the bathroom and wash up, but I still had on the same clothes.

Mrs. Reed and I were talking one day when she said that she had never seen such coldness in my eyes before. She hoped that I wouldn't do anything foolish.

I said to her, "It won't be foolish!" and I got up and walked over to Joy's bed. "How are you feeling, baby?"

"I'm so sore, but I'm feeling better. How do I look, Mark?"

"You look beautiful, baby."

"Mark, go home and get some rest. Clean up and change clothes. You've been here for three days now. I'm better. I'll be all right until you come back tomorrow. You can stay at Mom's house, in my old bedroom."

"Alright then, baby. I'm going to go. I'll be back tomorrow." The only thing on my mind was finding Butch and Leo. I wasn't going to rest until I did. The first place I stopped was by Eugene's house. I picked up Eugene. He gave me a .357 Magnum. He had a .45 automatic.

We drove over near Butch's house. We parked three blocks away and walked to the back of his house in the dark. There were no lights on in the house. It was still early. We knew that there was nobody home.

We waited in the bushes for about six hours, but it seemed like an eternity. Suddenly I heard someone whistling approaching. I whispered to Eugene, "I believe that's him coming now."

Sure enough, it was butch. He placed his key in the door to open it. We stepped from behind the bushes. He turned and looked. Surprised! But it was too late. I said, "Keep your hands on the door! Check him, Eugene."

Eugene pulled a .38 special from Butch's waistband and then stepped back.

"Alright, mother fucker, you can go on and open the door now and go on in so that we can have a discussion."

Once we got in, I turned on a light, then I asked, "Where is your bedroom?"

He pointed. I told him to go into it. We all went into the bedroom. I told him to get naked. He looked at me strangely and surprised. But he did exactly what I told him to do. Once he was completely naked, I saw that he was well hung. And that he must have really enjoyed punishing my woman. But tonight, he was going to experience the same agony.

I told him to put a pillow up under his stomach, and to lay on the bed spread eagle. Each arm and leg spread wide. I told Eugene to tie his hands and legs to the bed. Butch begged and pleaded with me. "Mark, don't do this. Please, don't do this to me."

I said, "Did you and your man enjoy my woman?"

He looked at me scared. "Mark, I'm sorry. I'm sorry, man. I shouldn't have listened to Leo. It was his idea."

"Was it Leo that split my woman's ass open and ruptured her insides?" All the while that I was talking, I was twisting three coat hangers together. I walked into the kitchen and turned on the stove. I reached into my pocket and pulled out a thick leather glove. I put it on and held the hangers over the fire until they were red hot.

I walked back into the bedroom and whipped his ass until sweat poured down my face. Eugene held his face into a pillow to muffle his screams. All the while that I beat him I said, "You are going to make a good little sex slave, aren't you?" Then I told Eugene to let his head up, long enough for him to answer.

He was crying out, "God, oh God, oh God, you are killing me."

"Answer my question."

"Yes, yes, I'll do anything that you say, only please, please don't beat me no more."

"Okay, I've got a horny friend for you to freak off with. I think this asshole is ready now."

"Eugene, go outside and bring that big German Shepherd that's tied up out back in here. This freak wants to suck his dick. Look at it this way, Butch, a dog gets a chance to suck a dog's dick and you won't stop until that dog gets off."

"Mark, I know that you are not serous. That's gross. You can't do a person like that!"

"Who said that you are a person. You're a dog. Look what you did to my woman!"

By that time, Eugene had come back into the bedroom with the huge dog.

"Now, before I have one of your hands untied, I'm going to let you know that I am very serious about this. I'm only going to tell you one time."

Then I stood at the end of the bed and took my .357 Magnum and broke both of his feet. As he screamed out in agony, Eugene once again muffled his voice with the pillow. I gave him a moment to compose himself as best he could, then I had Eugene untie one of his hands.

Eugene placed the shepherd on the bed in position over Butch's head. Butch looked at me. Tears were running down his face. "Don't do this to me," he cried.

I said, "This is your lucky night, man. Now get busy."

He immediately started sucking on the dog's dick. One of the dog's back legs started jerking. You could tell that the dog was enjoying the blowjob. The dog was making all types of funny sounds as the dog got off. We were standing there and I said, "You nasty bastard, you. You're not a man, you are a dog."

Then I noticed a pop bottle laying on the floor. "Eugene, place that pop bottle up his ass."

Eugene picked up the bottle and started pushing it up Butch's ass. Butch screamed so loud that Eugene stopped. I told him to hold the pillow over Butch's face. I took the heel of my foot and kicked the bottle all the way up his ass. Blood shot everywhere.

I then took my .357 Magnum, told Eugene to step back and I put two slugs into the back of his head.

Eugene shot him once and we walked back out into the darkness and made our way back to the car that was parked three blocks away.

I dropped Eugene off and told him that I would take care of Leo tomorrow. He asked if I needed any help with that. I told him, "No, I've got this." I went into Joy's mother's house and took a bath, laid in Joy's bed and fell asleep.

Chapter Eighteen

The next day I woke up and took a nice hot shower, went downstairs where Mrs. Reed had fixed a big breakfast for me. I ate and told her that I was going out to the hospital and spend some time with Joy.

She said for me to tell her that she would be out to see her later on. I said that I would and left.

As I entered Joy's room, she was sitting up in the bed. She had just finished eating breakfast herself. Her eyes lit up when she saw me. A big smile came over her face.

I said, "How is my beautiful black queen feeling today?"

She smiled and said, "Your queen is feeling much better. How is my handsome king feeling?"

"I'm feeling good knowing that you are feeling better." I bent over and kissed her on her sweet soft lips and said, "I love you."

"I know. I love you, too!"

We sat there and enjoyed each other and talked for the rest of the morning. At noon time, I told her that I wanted to watch the news.

"You love watching the news, don't you, baby?"

"Yes, I enjoy it. That's the only way that you are ever going to find out what's going on in your city and in the world." Then I got up and turned the TV on.

About five minutes into the news, they had a breaking story. The reporter was saying, "We are standing in front of a house at 1312 Michigan Avenue where a homicide had taken place within the last twelve hours. The coroner had reported the victim's name is Henry Philips, better known as 'Butch.'

"His brother came home an hour ago. The victim was completely naked laying on his stomach with each limb tied to the post of the bed. It appears there were multiple gunshot wounds to the back of his head and a gunshot wound to his side. It looked like a revenge killing, the police said, because the victim was sodomized with a large pop bottle forced up into his rectum. The detectives said that they would be investigating any similar crimes.

"The family is very distraught over the incident. They are all going to need support from each other."

Joy glanced away from the TV, looked towards me and smiled without saying a word.

I knew at that moment that she knew that I had avenged her honor. I had always respected women and for any man to violate a woman like they had violated my woman is not worthy of life!

My mind went directly to Leo. I knew that if he had seen the news that he would be trying to get out of town as quickly as possible. I then told Joy that I had to leave, but that I would be back later. I leaned over and kissed her.

"Be careful, baby," she said.

"I will. You just continue getting well," and I was out the door just that fast.

I was on my way to Eugene's. I was going to have him get out into the streets and help me locate Leo before he got away.

I was driving past the poolroom on Butler Street when I saw Leo coming out. Moving through the parking lot quickly, he was looking all around him. I swooped into the parking lot and jumped out of my car. As I jumped out, Leo noticed that it was me with gun in hand. He pulled a pistol out of his waistband. He was frantic. He fired a shot. He missed. The bullet hit my windshield. I returned two shots. Both hit its target. One shot hit him in the neck, the other in the chest. He was dead before he hit the ground.

I didn't even notice that the police were sitting across the street watching the whole thing. They swung over to the parking lot and jumped out of their car. One officer had a shotgun, the other had pulled his service revolver. I heard someone shout, "Drop your weapon!" I turned and saw that it was the police. I immediately dropped my weapon.

They ordered me to put my hands against the car. They handcuffed me and put me in the patrol car. By this time, the lot was filled with police. They took me to the police station and booked me for murder.

I wasn't in jail an hour before Goodman and Goldstein, both of my attorneys, came to see me. Mr. Goodman said, "Mark, what happened?"

I explained to him that the man shot at me first before I returned fire. Mr. Goldstein looked at Mr. Goodman and said, "When we leave here, we will walk on over to the prosecutor's office and get this charge dropped down to manslaughter, based on what Mark has told us, and we need to get the police report as well. But I'm sure that it is going to show that Mark has been overcharged.

We talked for over an hour before they left. They had told me that I might not get out until tomorrow at the arraignment. I asked the C.O. if he would give me a call. And he did. I called the hospital and told Joy what had just taken place. She started to cry. I told her, "It's gonna be alright!"

I asked her to call Tony and give him the rundown on what I just told her and that I should be out tomorrow. I told her that I loved her and we hung up.

Three months have passed since I've been out of jail. Joy has completely healed physically, but we were still working on the emotional part.

Tony and I had been quite busy with our many companies. Gerald had done a great job blowing the merchandise company up and I can't say enough about Mr. Davis running the jewelry stores and the diamond wholesale company. Joyce and Brenda always made sure that everything was running smoothly.

All I can say is that Tony and I have truly been blessed. Life has been good. The only obstacle in my way is this case. I was about to go to trial in a week. Joy had been really worrying about me. She had tried to blame herself a few times, but I always told her, "Sweetheart, you are not the blame. I can handle whatever it is that they come with, so always stay strong."

I was talking to Margo. She was worrying about me as well. She asked me what I thought would happen when I went to court. I told her that I'm sure that I'm going to get some time, but it's not going to be that much.

She asked me if I was worried about going to prison since I'd never been to prison before. I told Margo that I try not to worry about things over which I have no control. I just do what needs to be done.

A week had passed and it was October 2, 1978. It was the morning of my court appearance to be sentenced. Joyce, Tony and Brenda were all sitting in the courtroom.

My attorneys, Mr. Goodman and Mr. Goldstein, and I were sitting at the defense table. They were going over our procedures when the prosecutor, Mr. Black, came to our table. He leaned over and said to Mr. Goodman, "Two to five years, correct?"

"That's what we agreed on," said Mr. Goodman.

"You know that he's getting off easy, you owe me one," the prosecutor said, then he walked back to his table.

I looked over my shoulder and Joyce was staring forward at me with a worried look on her face. I smiled and winked at her to let her know that everything was alright. She smiled and winked back.

Then the bailiff said, "Everyone rise! The Honorable Judge Maggie Reynolds is presiding."

The judge said, "You may all be seated. This is Case CR-7623 versus Mark Jones charged with manslaughter. Now, my understanding is that there has been some type of agreement reached by the prosecutor's office with defense attorneys Goodman and Goldstein."

"That is correct, Your Honor," the prosecutor answered.

"And what is this agreement?" the judge asked.

"My office and the defense attorneys have agreed that if Mr. Jones plead guilty to reckless homicide, we will drop the manslaughter."

"Is that the agreement, Mr. Goodman, Mr. Goldstein?"

"Yes, Your Honor, that's the agreement."

"Then I will accept the agreement. Mr. Jones, do you understand that you have a right to a jury trial of your peers? If convicted, you have a right to appeal your conviction? By you pleading guilty, you are giving up all of those rights. Do you still want to plead guilty, Mr. Jones?"

"Yes, Your Honor," I answered.

"Do you have anything to say before sentencing, Mr. Jones?"

"No, Your Honor, I'm ready to get it over with."

"Very well, I sentence you to two to five years in state prison. The sentence is to go into effect immediately."

Two big deputies got up and were about to place handcuffs on me. Mr. Goodman asked, "Your Honor, I know that this is an unusual request, but may my client have one moment with his fiancé before he is escorted from the courtroom?"

The judge paused for a moment, then pulled her glasses down to the bridge of her nose and looked over them into the courtroom. She noticed this beautiful young lady sitting with tears running down her cheeks. She knew that she must be the fiancé. "Very well," she said, "Deputies, give them a few moments."

The deputies stepped back as Joyce was walking down the aisle. She stopped at the rail. She and I embraced and kissed. She said, "I love you, baby."

I said, "I love you, too, my beautiful queen!"

I told her to go back to Atlanta, and that I would let her know when I get to prison and when she could come and visit. I looked into the courtroom. Tony was standing there. He waved at me and said that he would take care of everyone. I knew that he meant Joy as well.

I winked at him to say, I know. I then said my goodbyes to Joyce and the deputies took me away.

I was only in jail a week when early one morning they called for me and four other guys to pack up and get ready to leave.

One of the men said, "This is it. We are on our way to the big house. It's no joke. I know. I've been there before. If you're not strong, you will be someone's woman. It's no place for the weak."

I looked over and saw this little guy that was leaving with us. I could see the fear in his eyes. I thought that he was going to break down and sob. I knew that he would belong to someone. It was just a matter of time.

The deputies started calling us out, one by one. They took us down to the holding pen and shortly thereafter to a waiting van.

The ride to the prison took over two hours. There was complete silence all the way there. When we approached the prison, one man said, "Look how tall those walls are."

The day that I entered into Michigan State Penitentiary was the beginning of a life like no other. I will never forget my first day behind those thick grey walls. There were gun towers all around the walls and in the center of the yard there stood a tall gun tower. I and the four other men were placed in the big block. This is where we were housed. It was six tiers high. None of us were put on the same tiers or the same cells.

It was very loud. The noise would last late into the night. Some guys would be singing out loud. Some would tell jokes and there would be laughter all through the cell block. Then I heard one guy holler, "Shut the fuck up, bitch!" and another guy say, "Who the fuck is you talking to?" "You're the one telling the jokes, aren't you?" he said to the man above us. "You're damn right I'm telling the jokes. You don't think they are funny?" "Hell no! That's why I said shut the fuck up, bitch!" The guy above said, "We'll see who the bitch is when the cell doors open in the morning."

This guy on my range even got stronger. He said, "Kiss my ass, mother fucker. Come on down here if you want to in the morning and you'll wish that you hadn't came."

I was lying in my bunk thinking to myself that this guy a couple of cells down from me must be a bad mother fucker.

The next morning the cell doors opened early. Now take it that these ranges are very long. There were men standing all the way down the range and it was very crowded. It all happened so fast. He was like a thief in the night. He came out of nowhere.

All I could see was the knife blade going in and out of this guy. Blood was squiring from his body as he was screaming, "Oh, God, help me. Please, help me. He's killing me." Blood was everywhere. This guy was a bloody mess.

I watched him as he died right in front of his cell. I heard him cough and blood gushed out of his mouth. That was the last sound that came from his limp body. Guards came running over ordering everybody back into their cells. I was celling with this Spanish guy. His name was Vasquez. He was from Chicago. He was busted in Detroit for bringing heroin.

All that day they interviewed every prisoner on the range on what happened and what they saw. I don't think that they got anything out of anyone. In state prison, if you snitch and if it's found out, you're dead!

Chapter Nineteen

Back in Atlanta, Tony was sitting in Margo's condo. Joy and Renee had just walked in. It was November 20th. I had been in prison for over a month.

Tony looked at Joy and asked, "Why are you looking so sad?"

"Because I miss my man and the holidays are coming up. In seven days, Thanksgiving will be here and I want to cook a big dinner for the both of us. I know that he would be at home on the holidays, but he would come and spend time with me also." Joy started to cry. "Tony, I miss Mark so much. I love him with all of my heart. He's the best thing to ever happen to me."

Renee reached over and hugged Joy. "Girl, Mark misses you, too, but he would want you to stay strong and enjoy the holidays."

Tony said, "That's right. Now that they have approved the visiting list, everybody can go and see him. I think that Joyce is going down this week. So we both can go the following week. I won't stay the whole visiting period. I know you guys need to have more time to yourselves. All I need to do is let Mark know what's going on with our businesses."

"Tony, you and Mark are so close and you work well together. It's good to see that in two friends," Margo said.

"He's not just my friend, Margo, he's my brother. At least that's the way that I feel about him. We may not be blood, but I wish we were 'cause I love Mark like a brother."

"Believe me, Tony, I understand. The trust you two have in each other."

"Listen, you guys, I've got to go. I've got a lot of work to do. Renee, baby, I'll see you tonight. Joy, we'll leave next week. Margo, you take care, little sis."

Everybody said bye and Tony was out the door.

Back in my cell...

My celly and I were sitting down playing cards. We had been cellies for over a month now. We didn't talk much about our cases, but later into our bit we would become close friends and learn much about one another.

At night we would lay in our bunks in the darkness of our cells and talk for hours about our women. I really liked him. He was a solid guy. He loved to talk about his goddess, as he would call his woman. I would tell him about Joyce and Joy and how good we are together. He asked me if they knew about one another? I said Joy knows about Joyce, but Joyce didn't know about Joy. And if she was to find out, it wouldn't make a difference because I'm the captain of my ship.

He laughed and said, "I like that confidence in you."

"Yeah, if a man don't run his, then he's no man." I also talked a lot about Tony. How cool we both were.

He would say, "Man, you guys are really close. I never had a friend like that."

Tony would write me often and keep me up on everything. He would bring Joy down to see me a lot. Sometimes Joy would come by herself. I had it arranged where Joyce and Joy never came the same weekends. I would get three to four letters a week from Margo as well. I didn't want for anything while in prison. I kept plenty of money on my books.

When they would have something good in the kitchen, I would have someone who worked in the kitchen steal it and bring it to my cell. Things like fried chicken, turkey, lunchmeat, whole pies. Whatever I liked, they would bring.

I would see Tommy, Dollar Bill and Curtis. We would all meet up on the yard. They would tell me that they couldn't wait to get out and go back to Lansing and open up the warehouse.

Many times we would all be in the visiting room at the same time. I was beginning to be like a celebrity in prison. My men always talked about Tony and me to the other prisoners and that would just give me more clout. There were many people in prison that knew us or of us and they knew to fuck with one of us was like signing their own death certificate.

I moved about with great respect. The time had gone past quickly. My men were getting ready to go home in another month. I would follow later.

Richard wasn't there when I first arrived at prison, so I never got a chance to see him. Dollar Bill had said that Richard had left about a month after they all had arrived. They had taken him to another prison.

It was now 1980 and I didn't have much to go. In a couple more months I would be out of here. Back into the world of freedom and I'm so damn happy about that.

Every day now my friend, Vasquez, and I would walk for a couple of hours on the large outside yard. The yard was so large. It had two baseball diamonds and a handball court and two basketball courts. You would see inmates playing these games every day. They would be all up in the bleachers and behind the baseball diamonds. They would be making bets on their favorite teams. You would think that these teams were professionals from the excitement that you would hear when someone would hit a home run on their favorite team. I often saw the little guy that came to prison with me that was about to cry before we left the county jail. He was with his man in the bleachers watching the game. He had been turned out to be a male prostitute turning tricks for his man. He would be all dolled up with Kool-Aid on his lips and blush on his cheeks. He wore a tee shirt torn off at the waist and tied in a knot in the front with some short shorts. I heard that they call the little guy "Sugar." He would turn as many as five to ten tricks a day. I heard rumors that he would cry out, "Fuck me, Daddy. Fuck me good," whenever someone would turn a trick with him.

His man would have cartons of cigarettes stacked everywhere in his cell from his male bitch. The cellblock had just come back from dinner and the cells were still open. My celly and I had decided to play some cards.

When I heard a scream in the next cell, I looked at my celly and he looked at me. I said, "Hell, they must be killing the guy next door." I stood up and went out on the range and peeped into the cell next to me. They had a blanket draped over the bed, hanging down from the top bunk. This white guy jumped out butt naked. A black guy jumped out after him. He said, "Get your ass back in the bed, bitch!"

I looked and saw blood dripping down from the white boy's ass onto the floor. He looked at me and said, "Man, he busted my ass, he busted my ass."

The black guy told him, "Get your ass back into that bed. Ain't nothing wrong with your mouth." At that moment, I turned and went back into my cell.

Another time I was down on the first range where we took our showers. A shower cubicle had about eight shower stems in it. It was tight. You couldn't bend over and wash your legs or feet without hitting someone's dick. You do the best that you can.

Normally, the white guys showered in one cubicle and the black guys showered in another on the other side of the cellblock.

Well, one particular night, a new white guy wanting to shower came into the black shower. Everyone looked at him strangely, but didn't say a word. The man started washing his hair. He lathered his hair up good. His eyes were closed to keep the soapsuds out. That's when some guys grabbed him by both of his arms. Other guys quickly left the shower room so that someone could grab both of his legs. A great big man grabbed him by his head bending him over.

One guy lathered up his whole hand and I believe that he ran his whole hand up the white boy's ass by the scream that the man let out. They took turns fucking this guy. When they finally released him, he could barely walk. He walked very wide legged.

The rest of my time was spent in my cell, reading and meditating, preparing myself for my release back into the free world. I had been locked up for eighteen months now. It was well worth it. I had avenged the abuse that Butch and Leo had taken my woman through. Now all of this was behind me and my freedom before me at last.

Betty had been writing me for the last five to six months. She had seen Joy in Lansing and had told her that I was in prison and had given her my address. Joy was back in Lansing visiting her family. I had just gotten a letter from Betty a few days before it was time for me to get released. She said that she had left the prosecutor's office and that she was in private practice now. It was a small office and she didn't have that many clients, but she was comfortable and she was glad to get away from that racist prosecutor Hindenburg. She said that she had seen and heard too much about how they were abusing and setting up black people. She said that she couldn't stay there any longer.

I wrote back that once I came home, she could come and work for Tony and me on the legal side. If she liked that, we could set her up with her own firm.

The day finally came for me to leave. As I was at the front desk signing my papers and picking up my money to go home, I noticed Joyce sitting there smiling, waiting on me. She got up, and as she was walking towards me, two big white detectives walked up and said, "Mark Jones, we have a warrant for your arrest for first-degree murder."

I said, "Murder, who in the hell am I supposed to have killed?"

"Mr. Raymond Little. You do remember a Mr. Raymond Little, don't you? Better known as Slim."

"I didn't kill Slim."

"You can straighten that out when you get back to Lansing. All I know is that we are supposed to bring you in."

Joyce started crying. "Baby, what's going on? What are they talking about?"

"Call Tony now, baby, and tell him to have my lawyer waiting on me when I get back to Lansing."

One of the detectives said, "Come on, it's time to go, Mr. Jones."

Joyce shouted out, "I love you, Mark!"

"I love you too, baby," I shouted back. I was devastated. I didn't understand what was happening.

All the way back, my mind was going a hundred miles an hour. Once we were back in Lansing, and I was booked, my lawyer was waiting on me. They led me into this little room where both Goodman and Goldstein were waiting.

"Have a seat, Mark," said Goodman.

I said, "What the hell is going on?"

"It's some guy named Richard James. He said that you hired him and Jerome Edwards to kill Raymond Little. He's a witness for Prosecutor Roland Hindenburg."

The name immediately rang a bell in my head. This was the man that Betty used to work for that has been railroading black men into prison. This guy is a liar and a crook himself.

"I don't know what the hell this guy is talking about! I didn't pay this guy, Richard, to do anything for me. How can they charge me with murder on his word? He's a convicted felon himself. All I want to know is what makes him so damned credible?"

"Mark, we are on your side. Mr. Goldstein and I both agreed with everything that you just said, but the way that they are trying to tie this thing together is, I don't know if you remember back some time ago when you met Slim on Butler Street at the bar-b-que joint, he was with this man called Joe. You shook Slim's hand and Joe's hand and Slim handed you some money."

"Yeah, I remember. But the money wasn't for me. It was for one of my friends. He asked me to give it to him."

"That may be true," Mr. Goodman said, "but here's the problem. That guy Joe, his whole name is Joseph Shelton, he's a narcotics detective, and what they are saying is that you sold Slim some heroin on the porch that night and that Joe witnessed the sale. You must have found out later that Slim was a confidential informer and that Joe was a cop. That supposedly is your motive for having Slim killed, or so Prosecutor Hindenburg says. Now we know that he is fabricating this story that you had sold drugs that night just to pin this murder on you. We've got to discredit this whole myth! But this is going to take time. The way that I look at it, your trial may not start for at least six months. We'll be going to the courtroom tomorrow for them to read off the charges. Just going through the formalities."

"Listen, Mr. Goodman, what are my chances of getting bond when we go into court?"

"To be honest, Mark, very slim! But we will ask just the same."

"So what you are saying is that I'm going to have to sit in jail until this thing is over?"

"Yes, that's what I'm saying, Mark."

"Do you think that we can win this, Mr. Goodman?"

Mr. Goodman paused for a moment and he looked at Mr. Goldstein and said, "We are gonna damn sure do our best! It's going to be a tough one. This prosecutor has the deck stacked against us with their snitch and their detective. We've got to discredit these guys some kind of way and show the jury that they are no more than liars."

"Well, I heard that this prosecutor likes railroading black men into prison, is that true?"

"Yes, Mark. There have been a lot of complaints against him, but no one has been able to prove it."

"Then we have to try to find something out on him. I don't care whatever it takes, if we have to hire private investigators, I don't care, do it. Tony will pay for it all."

"We'll see what we can do. I'll see you in court tomorrow, Mark."

We all stood up. I shook Mr. Goodman and Mr. Goldstein's hands. Mr. Goldstein put his hand on my shoulder and said, "Mark, we are going to do everything in our power to win this thing."

Chapter Twenty

I had been sitting in jail for four months now and we were still not ready for trial. My lawyers have been filing all kinds of motions, trying to get the case dismissed before going to trial, but nothing had worked.

We even filed a motion of discovery to see what all the prosecutor had against me. The only thing that made his case strong was that he had snitch ass Richard saying that I paid him and Jerome to take Slim out. They also had this cop that was setting the stage by saying that I sold Slim some dope and that I found out that Slim was an informant. That was my motive for having Slim killed.

Here I was between a rock and a hard place. My lawyers still hadn't come up with anything. It was now August 30, 1980.

Betty came to see me a few times already. She asked is there was anything that she could do to help. I told her thanks, but I had two very good experienced trial lawyers and if I had any chance of winning it, it would be with both of them. Betty really wanted to help. She lowered her head and when she raised it back up, I saw a sadness in her eyes that I had never seen before. She was a beautiful person and she was going to make a hell of an attorney one day. I gave her a rundown on what her old boss was trying to do to me. She said, "That was one of the reasons that I left his office. The way that he would talk about our people. He would use the word nigger and coon often. He didn't care if I was present or not. Detectives would come in with virtually nothing against many young black men and they would sit there and discuss different strategies to send them to prison. This guy is evil, he is no earthly good."

I asked her if she had anything that could prove that he had railroaded so many black men into prison.

"I wish I did," she said, "but I don't. All I have is my word. And you know that's not good enough when it comes to white people doing something to black folks, Mark."

I told her that sometimes it seems like we are still in the 50s and 60s in the south. The only difference is that they keep their racism on the down low these days.

I told her not to worry and that things would work out. "These crackers may have me down, but I'm not out yet. There is still a lot of fight left in me," I said.

We talked for about a half hour more. We hugged. Then we said our goodbyes and she walked away. The C.O. escorted me back to my cellblock.

When I walked in, all of the men were occupying themselves by playing spades or chess. Some were watching TV.

I, myself, immediately went to my cell and sat on my bunk wondering if my lawyers would be able to win my case.

Here I am from the prison I once lived in for eighteen months only to emerge into a cell in the county jail. Fate had dealt me a cold hand. From one set of struggles I entered into another.

The prosecutor and the detectives have put together an elaborate scheme to frame me. My life hangs on a string. My head was beginning to hurt. I decided to lay back and get me some rest.

It was December 10, 1980. I had been in jail for eight months. My trial was to start on January 5th. It will be 1981.

I was waiting on my man, Tony, to come and visit me today. Joyce was here yesterday, and Joy was here the day before.

I heard the C.O. yell out my name. "Jones, you have a visitor."

I checked myself out in the mirror and followed the C.O into the visiting room. I saw Tony sitting at a table in the back. The visiting room was filled with inmates and their loved ones. When I got to the table, Tony got up and gave me a hug. He asked me how I was doing. I said, that I was good under the circumstances.

"Sit down, Mark," Tony said.

"Tony, be honest with me. What does it look like to you? Do you think I have a chance?"

"There is always a chance. I talked to Goodman and Goldstein. They said the whole thing is convincing the jury that the snitch, the detective and the prosecutor are all out to get you and that everything is a big lie!"

"But can they convince the jury, Tony?"

Tony bit his bottom lip, folded his hands on the table and looked at me. He shook his head and said, "I don't know. Mark, I just don't know. I even asked Mr. Goodman if the judge would take some money. We'd give him whatever he wants, a hundred thousand, five hundred thousand, whatever it took. Mr. Goodman said not only would the judge not accept the money, but he would be convinced that everything that the snitch, the detective and the prosecutor said is true!"

"Damn, Tony. This shit don't look good. There's got to be a way to get out of this shit."

"Yeah, Mark, we're going to fight like hell."

"The trial starts next month. I'm kind of anxious to get it started. So Tony, when are you going back to Atlanta?"

"I'm going to leave next week, Mark. Then I'm coming right back here. I am going to stay here until your trial is over, then we are going to go back together."

I smiled because Tony and I were so close. And if I lose this case, he would stop at nothing to bribe anyone and everyone that he could to get me out of prison. Even the governor, if it would cost a million dollars. He would pay it.

We continued with our visit. We didn't talk anymore about my case. We talked about when we first met many years ago and all that we've been through together. Things that we did, some silly, most serious. We sat there and laughed and just enjoyed our visit. We talked about our women and how lucky we were to have two women apiece that were truly in our corners.

He gave me a rundown on how good our companies were doing and that we were getting wealthier and wealthier as each year passed by.

I came from one of the lowest points in my life when I first met Tony, and to achieve much success only to wind up in jail fighting for my life, not able to enjoy all that I've accomplished over these many years.

What a waste if I don't win my case. Shortly after, Tony left and I went back to my cell.

January 5, 1981 finally arrived. It was the beginning of my trial. We picked my jury. There wasn't much to chose from, mostly all white. We did manage to get one black woman on my jury. She was an older black woman with salt and pepper hair. She had very kind eyes. If nothing else, maybe she might hang up my jury because the white folks on the jury are looking at me like I'm guilty already. And the trial hasn't even started yet.

The lawyers on both sides had their opening arguments. The prosecutor was talking to the jury, talking about how he would prove that I was guilty beyond a reasonable doubt, that I may not have pulled the trigger myself, but that I am just as guilty because I paid someone to do my dirty work. He told them if it wasn't for my blood money, Mr. Raymond Little would still be alive today. Then he walked over to the jury box and laid both hands on the rail and he looked them in the eyes. As his eyes traveled up and down into everyone's face, he said, "For that reason, and that reason alone, ladies and gentlemen of the jury," then he quickly turned and pointed his finger directly at me, "you should find Mr. Mark Jones guilty of first-degree murder!

"Now if by some reason, you choose to let this killer go free, then give me one hour to pack my family up so that I can leave this state because this state is no longer safe for me and my family to live in." Then the bastard walked back to his table and took a seat.

My attorney, Mr. Goldstein, addressed the jury. "Ladies and gentlemen of the jury, I am here to prove today that everything the prosecutor and his informant have to say about my client, Mr. Jones, is a fabricated lie that they concocted. Prosecutor Hindenburg should be in the theater because he put on a good performance. I don't have a problem with his acting, because I know that you ladies and gentlemen of the jury are intelligent enough to weigh the facts and see through a lie." Mr. Goldstein turned and walked back to the table and sat down.

It was a week of intense arguments. Every day Tony, Brenda and Joyce would be in the courtroom. Everything was looking pretty good until the prosecutor called his next witness.

From a side door next to the judge's chambers, Richard came walking out. He looked at me then his eyes dropped to the floor as he took the stand.

The bailiff asked him to raise his right hand and to swear to tell the truth and nothing but the truth, and he did.

They asked him to state his full name for the record.

"Richard James."

"Mr. James, do you know that man sitting at the defense table wearing the gray silk suit?"

"Yes, sir."

"And what is his name?"

"Mark Jones."

"And how do you know Mark Jones?"

"I met him through my friend, Jerome."

"And where were you when you met him?"

"I was at Jerome's house."

"What did you all talk about?"

"He wanted to pay us to kill someone for him."

"Who did he want killed?"

"A guy named Slim."

"Is this Slim also Raymond Little?"

"Yes, it is."

"So, did you and Jerome kill Slim?"

"Yes, we kidnapped him and ran into the police unexpectedly. It was a shootout and I shot and killed Slim and exited the vehicle. At that time I was shot several times."

They continued on for about forty-five minutes more. I was sitting there stunned in disbelief in what I was hearing. I had never met with this man and he was sitting there on the stand just as calm, lying through his teeth.

It was like a dream that turned into a nightmare. Now it was my lawyer's turn to get up and ask the questions. Mr. Goodman got up, put his glasses on the bridge of his nose and walked toward Richard.

"Good afternoon, Mr. James. I know that you must be getting a little tired up there on the stand so I'll try not to hold you as long as Prosecutor Hindenburg did."

Then Mr. Goodman smiled at Richard. Richard smiled back, but all the time, Mr. Goodman knew that he was a piece of scum and he was about to break him down.

"Mr. James, you said that you killed Mr. Little, is that correct?"

"Yes, sir!"

"How much time are you serving, Mr. James?"

"I am serving a fifteen to life sentence."

"And how much time will you have to do before you are eligible for parole?"

"Thirteen years, sir."

"So you've got thirteen reasons to sit there and tell a lie on Mr. Jones!"

"No, sir."

"No, sir, you don't have thirteen reasons?"

"No, sir, I am not lying on Mr. Jones."

"Well, Jerome certainly can't tell us what happened 'cause he's dead! Mr. James, did the prosecutor offer you anything for your testimony against Mr. Jones?"

Mr. James glanced over at the prosecutor as if to get approval to answer the question.

Mr. Goodman said, "I don't know why you are looking at Mr. Hindenburg. Just answer my question."

"Would you repeat the question, sir?"

"I asked you if you were offered anything for your testimony."

He looked back at Mr. Hindenburg. Hindenburg nodded giving Mr. James the okay to answer the question.

"Yes, sir, I was told that I would get credit for the time that I've served and get immediate release for my testimony right after this trial is over."

"Now isn't that something! A convicted murderer will be set free just for helping to convict an innocent man!"

My trial was now in its third week and things are not looking good. We really didn't have anything to work with. The court was in recess. That gave me a chance to discuss my case with my lawyers. I turned to my attorney, Mr. Goodman, and asked what his next move was.

"There is nothing left in my arsenal. It doesn't look good. I don't know what to tell you. I'm sorry. Maybe we should concentrate more on your appeal."

"Are you telling me that you believe that we are going to lose this?"

"Yes, Mark, we didn't have much to work with from the beginning. Look at that jury. I can't remember when the last time I've seen a jury look more convinced. It's as if Mr. James and the prosecutor cannot tell a lie."

"But he's a convicted murderer!"

"That is true, Mark, but the jury believes if the prosecutor uses him as a witness that he's credible or he wouldn't use him. See, people that have never been in trouble with the law are so naïve, they believe that if you are arrested for something, you must have done it.

Chapter Twenty-One

The judge came back into the courtroom and took his seat on the bench. He then asked, "Are both sides ready to proceed?"

The prosecutor said, "The prosecution is ready."

Mr. Goodman said, "Your Honor, may I have one moment with my client?"

"Yes, but make it quick," the judge said.

My attorney said, "I have nothing else, Mark, I think we should close."

I turned and looked at Mr. Goldstein. He said, "I think that we need to concentrate on your appeal. There is no need for us to keep pulling for straws when there is nothing there."

I leaned back in my seat. Thoughts were moving through my head so fast, wondering to myself what I was paying these guys all of this money for?

Mr. Goldstein interrupted my thoughts. He said, "Mark, I am going to go ahead and close." He stood up and said, "Your Honor, we are going to...

At that moment, the doors opened in the back of the courtroom. Betty was walking down the aisle with elegance and grace. She had on a blue business suit and a briefcase in her hand. She had a confident look on her face.

At that moment, it seemed like every eye in the courtroom was on her as she moved gracefully toward us.

"Your Honor, my name is Attorney Betty Cobbs and I am here to help represent Mr. Jones!"

Betty walked through the swinging gates and stood right behind me. She put her hands on my shoulders.

The judge asked, "Is that correct, Mr. Jones? Is she one of your attorneys?"

I leaned my head back and looked into Betty's eyes.

She said, "Mark, let me do this. I feel that I can win this."

I thought to myself, what the hell, what do I have to lose? I said, "Yes, Your Honor, this is one of my attorneys."

She asked the judge for a few moments to confer with the other attorneys. The judge granted it.

Mr. Goodman immediately said, "Mark, she's not experienced with trying a murder case."

"Well, she can't do any worse than what y'all have done."

Betty started looking through the notes on the desk. Afterward she told the judge that she was ready to proceed.

"Your Honor, I have three witnesses to call to the stand and after that, I have three more to prove that they are liars. Your Honor, for my first witness, I'd like to call Mr. Richard James back to the stand."

"Mr. James, you have already been sworn in," the court bailiff said.

"Mr. James, at any time while you were arrested, did Sergeant Frederick or Detective Winfield ever come and question you about Mark Jones?"

"No, ma'am!"

"So you are saying that neither detective came and questioned you about Mark Jones?"

"That is correct."

"What about Prosecutor Hindenburg? Did he ever ask if Mark Jones paid you to kill Raymond Little?"

"No, ma'am."

"No, ma'am, he never came to interview you?"

"That is correct."

"So neither of these men that I asked about asked you to lie about Mark Jones and that they would make it easier on you?"

"That's right."

During her questioning of Mr. James, I noticed that Prosecutor Hindenburg and Sergeant Frederick were smiling.

"Mr. James, I have no further questions. You may step down. Your Honor, for my next witness, I would like to call Sergeant Frederick to the stand."

After being sworn in, she began her questioning. "Detective, how long have you been on the Lansing, Michigan police force?"

"It will be seventeen years this coming June."

"In your seventeen years, have you ever lied, coerced or framed anyone to get a conviction?"

"No, I haven't!"

"Did you or Detective Winfield ever try to get Richard James to lie and say that Mark Jones paid him to kill Raymond Little?"

"No, ma'am, that is not how the law works."

"I didn't say that's how the law works. I asked if you or Detective Winfield ever asked Richard James to lie on Mark Jones?"

"No, ma'am, we haven't."

"Have you or Detective Winfield or both of you ever interviewed Richard James with prosecutor Hindenburg?"

"No, ma'am."

"That's good. So I guess that you are the officers that do everything right?"

"Well, we try to be fair at all times."

"So you are fair officers?"

"That's right, ma'am."

"That is very interesting, fair officers that go by the book. I see. You may step down, Detective Frederick."

Sergeant Frederick stepped down and looked at the prosecutor and winked his eye. Then he walked over and took his seat.

"Your Honor, my next witness is Prosecutor Hindenburg."

"For God's sakes, Your Honor, you are not going to continue to allow this young lady to make a mockery of the court?"

"Your Honor, I'm not trying to make a mockery of the court. I am trying to keep my client from doing life for a murder that he had no part in. And I will prove it shortly."

"Very well," the judge said. "Prosecutor Hindenburg, take the stand."

The prosecutor palmed both hands on the table and got up with a disgusted look on his face and took the stand. He was sworn in and Betty began her questioning.

"I know that you don't want to be sitting there and I won't hold you as long as I held the others. Sir, do you know me?" Betty asked the prosecutor.

"Of course I know you, you used to work for me."

"And what type of work did I do for you when I worked for you in your office?"

"You would keep our records and you worked in the evidence room making sure that everything was in its proper place. And you would destroy everything that was no longer needed."

"Did I ever prosecute a case?"

"You would co-prosecute cases to gain experience."

"Would you say that I'm an honest person?"

Prosecutor Hindenburg leaned back in his chair, rubbed his nose and said, "Yes, that's fair to say. You're honest."

"Thank you, sir. Mr. Hindenburg, have you ever questioned Richard James with Sergeant Frederick and Detective Winfield? And did you ever ask him to lie and say that Mr. Mark Jones hired him to kill Raymond Little?"

"No, I never did and I wouldn't do anything like that. Where are you going with this preposterous line of questioning? Earlier in the trial you said that you had three witnesses that were going to prove that your first three witnesses were liars. I guess the two detectives and I are the first three witnesses. Where are your second three witnesses? They are probably no more than common criminals and liars. If they get up here and tell a lie, I am going to have them charged with perjury!"

"Very well, sir, I have no further questions. You may step down. Your Honor, I would like to bring my next witnesses forward, but I will need a tape recorder."

The judge leaned forward in his seat and said, "A tape recorder?"

"Yes, Your Honor, because I have my next three witnesses on tape. Actually, Your Honor, there are four witnesses."

"Very well." The judge ordered the bailiff to set up a tape recorder on the defense attorney's table. Betty walked over to the table.

I asked, "What's going on, Betty? What do you have?"

She said, "Sit back, Mark, and enjoy the show. You are going to love this."

Both attorneys, Mr. Goodman and Mr. Goldstein, were wondering in their minds. Wondering what on earth this young inexperienced attorney could possibly have that would set me free. But they had to admit to themselves that she had argued my case very well so far.

Betty took the tape out of her briefcase and placed it into the tape recorder. She turned to the judge and the jury and said, "Your Honor, ladies and gentlemen of the jury, what you are about to listen to now will prove beyond a reasonable doubt that my client had nothing to do with the murder of Raymond Little! And it will also prove that all these men that I just questioned had conspired to send my client to prison for something that he had nothing to do with. I am going to start the tape now, Your Honor."

The tape started to play. The first words came out of the tape.

"Mr. James, you know why we are here. And this is a chance for you to save your ass! You are facing life here if convicted of the murder of Raymond Little! Now your friend, Jerome Edwards, is dead. So if you help us put Mark Jones away, we will probably be able to get you a five to fifteen year sentence. That will be a manslaughter charge!" Sergeant Frederick said. "Is that correct Prosecutor Hindenburg?"

"Yes, that's correct."

"So what do you say, Mr. James. Are you ready to work with us?"

"What is it that you want me to do?" Mr. James asked.

"We want you to say that it was Mark Jones that gave you the contract to kill Raymond Little."

The jury was astounded. You could see the emotions on their faces. I knew what they were thinking. How could someone that was sworn to uphold the law break the law and try to send an innocent man to prison. The tape continued.

"Well, sir, I can't do that. Nobody gave us a contract to kill this man. It was a dispute over some money that he and Jerome had."

"Listen, you black asshole, I'm tired of fooling around with you. If you don't say that Mark Jones gave you the contract to kill Raymond Little, your ass is going down. You will never see daylight again."

Richard James said, "Sergeant, what you are asking me to do is lie."

"You're damn right, you sonofabitch!" Prosecutor Hindenburg said. "Is that tape recorder running?"

"Yes, it's running," Detective Winfield said.

"Then turn that damn thing off!"

Betty then clicked off the recorder and walked over by the jury and said, "All I want you to do is search your hearts for the truth. The facts have been laid out in this case and now it is up to you, the jury, to decide who to believe. You've just heard with your own ears the two detectives and the prosecutor threatening Richard James by telling him that he would never see daylight again if he didn't lie and say that Mark Jones hired him and Mr. Edwards to kill Mr. Little.

"I know that at the beginning many of you probably had your minds made up that these two officers and this prosecutor wouldn't get on the stand and raise their right hand and swear to tell the truth. Then as you've heard, tell a lie! I feel that the ones that need to be punished are the ones that conspired to send an innocent man to prison! The only thing that's worse than having a guilty man get off free is to have an innocent man convicted of a crime in which he had no part.

"With that, I close and I trust that you, ladies and gentlemen of the jury, will come back with the right verdict."

Prosecutor Hindenburg got up and made his closing argument. It was brief. He knew that his case had fallen apart after the audio tape was played. He and the two detectives were sitting at the table nervously as the jury left the room to deliberate.

Betty sat down at the defense table. She asked, "How did I do?"

I told her that I thought she did a great job and that I was proud of her.

She smiled as she cuffed my hand with both of her hands and said, "Thank you, Mark, I hope I made a difference."

"I'm sure you did, Betty."

Mr. Goodman asked Betty, "Where did you get the tape?"

She said that when she was leaving the prosecutor's office that she wanted to get out of there so fast that she accidentally threw some of their things into her box. The box had been sitting in her closet all this time. She said that she was straightening her closet out a couple of days ago. When she was going through the box, she noticed this tape and decided to play it. She recognized the voices and they were trying to set me up.

Mr. Goldstein said, "Well, I'll be damned! What are the chances that she would accidentally grab that tape and throw it in her box?"

"Hell, I don't know, what, one in a million?" Mr. Goodman said.

We all started to laugh."

"I'm just glad she found it." I looked over my shoulder and Joyce and Tony were sitting there. Tony gave me a thumbs up. I read Joyce's lips. She said, "Baby, you are coming home with me today!"

The officer came over and told me that we had to go into the back until the jury came back with their verdict. I was back there for about two hours before the jury came back with their verdict. When I came back into the courtroom, all of my lawyers were sitting at the table. I sat down between my lawyers. Betty was on my right. She was looking a little worried.

I said, "Betty, don't worry. You did a good job."

Mr. Goodman whispered to me, "It's too fast, Mark, that's not a good sign."

I looked over toward the prosecutor's table. I saw him and the two detectives start to get their confidence back that they had won.

Then the judge asked, "Ladies and gentlemen of the jury, have you reached a verdict?"

"Yes, we have, Your Honor."

"Would you hand your verdict to the bailiff."

They handed the verdict to the bailiff and the bailiff handed the verdict to the judge. The judge looked over the verdict and handed it back to the bailiff. The judge asked my attorneys and me to rise. He asked the jury, "Are you sure this is your verdict?"

Every member of the jury said yes. Then the bailiff read the verdict.

"On the charge of murder in the first degree, the jury finds you, Mark Jones, not guilty!"

Joyce couldn't hold her emotions. She screamed out, "Oh, my God, I told you, baby. I told you that you were coming home!"

The judge said, "Mr. Jones, you are free to go."

I said, "May I address the court, Your Honor, before I leave?"

"Yes, you may, Mr. Jones."

"Thank you, Your Honor. First, I'd like to thank you, ladies and gentlemen of the jury, for rendering a fair and just verdict and for seeing through the lies and deceit that the prosecutors and the two detectives were trying to put over on you. I always live my life by principles and morals. I always tried to keep my values right. And if by chance I stray, it's not because I planned it that way, it's because it just happened.

"I have never intentionally tried to bring harm to another person, just for the sake of bringing myself up to another level. Many times through my life I have run across obstacles, but those, I have always managed to overcome. Life can be confusing at times and we don't always make the right decisions. But this day is a good day for me, because you all, ladies and gentlemen of the jury, have made the right decision.

"I thank you and that is all, Your Honor."

Betty started to cry.

I said, "Betty, we won."

"I know, Mark, I'm just so happy and your speech was so beautiful."

"Thank you, baby. You did one hell of a job yourself."

"Mark, you spoke well today," said Mr. Goodman.

Both of my attorneys turned to Betty and congratulated her on what a fine job she'd done and told her if she ever wanted to come and work at their firm that she would be welcomed.

We all started to leave. As we were walking down the aisle, my beautiful queen Joyce was standing there. I put my arm around her shoulder and with my other hand, I wiped away the tears that were rolling down her cheeks. I kissed her sweet soft lips and said, "Let's get out of here, baby. I told you, it's gonna be alright!"

Epilogue

Three years have passed. It is now 1984. Life has had its ups and downs. Two years ago, my woman Joy, my angel, was in a terrible car accident. She died hours later at the hospital.

I'm still dealing with the trauma of losing her. It has had a devastating effect on me. My heart has been heavy with grief, but it's getting better. I know she would want me to live life to the fullest so that is what I'm trying to do.

My beautiful black queen, Joyce, and I got married in 1983. I hold her close to my heart, this woman I love very much. We had a big extravagant wedding. Tony, my partner, and Brenda also got married a couple of months later.

Tony and I now own four jewelry stores, a diamond wholesale business and two warehouses of which Gerald is still the president.

Margo and Renee are still working at the warehouse and loving it.

Eugene, Tommy, Curtis and Dollar Bill own their own merchandise warehouse in Lansing. Their company is doing very well. They purchase all of their merchandise from us.

Prosecutor Hindenburg, Sergeant Frederick and Detective Winfield were charged and convicted of perjury. They were all given sentences of two to five years in state prison.

Richard's plea agreement was honored and he was released. However, three weeks after his release, he was found tied spread eagle on a bed naked. He had multiple gunshot wounds to the head and body. A large object was inserted into his rectum. A large male dog was found standing over him.

Betty is now a full partner at Goodman, Goldstein and Cobbs. Her clientele has grown since winning my case. Everyone wants to hire her.

We talk on the phone at least a couple times a month long distance.